T0273573

The historical novel, an excellent entrée into the study of history, is quite in vogue these days. But in this fascinating new novel by Christina Eastwood that deals with the origin of evolutionism, a set of characters appear that one virtually never sees in this genre: English Particular Baptists. What a delight to read and see the depictions of these men and women about whom I have written at great length and thought much more. I was especially delighted that the missionary William Ward, the bicentennial of whose death is being remembered this year (he died in 1823), has a major role in this book. Highly recommended for young adults.

—**Michael A.G. Azad Haykin**
Professor of Church History
The Southern Baptist Theological Seminary

Dr Darwin's
ASSISTANT

Dr Darwin's ASSISTANT

Christina Eastwood

RITCHIE
John Ritchie Publishing

40 Beansburn, Kilmarknock, Scotland

ISBN-13: 978 1 914273 40 7

Copyright © 2023 by John Ritchie Ltd
40 Beansburn, Kilmarnock, Scotland
www.ritchiechristianmedia.co.uk

Typeset by John Ritchie Ltd., Kilmarnock
Printed by Bell & Bain Ltd., Glasgow

To Lucy Hope Jones

There's only one blessing, there's only one song,
There's only one path we can travel along,
There's only one road up to heaven above,
It's the road that was opened by Jesus' great love.
O may that sweet blessing now rest on your head,
And may that safe path be the one that you tread.
O come to the Saviour, may He be your song,
And own Him your Captain through all your life long.

With love from
Nain

Contents

Chapter One

FULL STREET

1859 and 1792

Hear him ye Senates! hear this truth sublime,
"He, who allows oppression, shares the crime."

*(Erasmus Darwin, The Botanic Garden. Part II.
Containing The Loves of the Plants. A Poem.
With Philosophical Notes.)*

hideous mantle clock is ticking away the seconds of 1859 and of the eighty-fourth year of my life. The fire is blazing: I feel the cold intensely these days. The small table beside me is littered with missionary magazines and pamphlets and thinly veiled appeals; appeals for funds for evangelising chimney-sweeps and guttersnipes; for Bibles for gypsies, road menders, mill workers and for special workhouse editions.

I close the well-bound new book, this so-called *Origin of Species,* and put it down on the side table with a bang that sends *Missionary Labours Among the Irish Navvies* and *Gospel Tidings for Tenement Dwellers* fluttering down to the hearthrug. I subscribe to all these things as liberally as I can, I think to myself testily. Why have they allowed this weed to flourish among them? Don't they see it will poison their efforts; destroy their message? What's the use in telling the canal boatman, "Jesus died for your sin" if all the other voices have already convinced him there is no such thing? What's the use if all the other voices – the squire and the magistrate, the don and the parson – have already convinced him that human beings are only the pinnacle of creation in the sense that they have fought and struggled and destroyed until everything else is beneath them? If he is already convinced that this hideous progress by slaughter is right – the only right? In all this time why have not they ...?

They? We ...? I ...? Matthew Batchelor? I pause, even in the flow of my righteous grumpiness: I have known this idea to be utterly false for over sixty years.

I take up the book again: *On the Origin of Species by Means of Natural Selection, or the Preservation of Favoured Races in the*

Struggle for Life by my old master's grandson, lent to me by my very young friend, the vicar. "Well reasoned, interesting research. Promising young scientist, very promising. You'll enjoy it – being a medical man yourself."

He seemed surprised when I told him I'd read it already in the poetic version by the author's grandfather and I'd considered it stuff and nonsense for the best part of my over-long life. Then I had to apologise for my gruffness and blame it on my gouty foot.

I feel bad tempered still. I know what I ought to do and my tired old body revolts against the thought of so much labour. With difficulty I haul myself out of the fireside chair. I reach for my stick and hobble to the huge old writing desk that comes, like me, from another era. I gather pens, paper, ink. I rummage in the bookcase and dig out my old master's books of poems. If I have to write I'll head every single chapter with a quotation from his verbose, pompous, overblown verses, I think to myself irritably. Then I wonder if I can write anything now other than, "Two spoonfuls to be taken in water twice daily ... dissolve the powder in liquid and administer as required ..."

I dip my pen in the inkwell, determined to make a start. Briefly, I commit the undertaking to God, knowing that only He can give me the strength to complete what I should have begun years ago. I gather my scattered thoughts for a moment and to my surprise the old characters and personalities from the far distant past come crowding into clear focus in my mind. I shake my head, almost in disbelief. Then my pen begins to crawl its way slowly across the paper. In the wavering hand of an old, old man, I trace out the most important episode in my life and the blank sheets start to teem with life.

It was comfortable in the kitchen in Full Street despite a wild March gale howling down the chimney and the cold rain hurling itself at the windows. Stout Mrs B had been baking and I was sampling the results. I was at that heroic age when somehow a lad is always hungry and kindly Mrs B was understanding. She was well aware from personal experience that those who grow up without much food are apt to be fond of it all their life. And I had certainly grown up in a situation where there was no food to spare.

My late grandmother had lived in the poorest part of Derby town, not far from Mrs B's own birthplace. Since the time she had lost my grandfather and all her money with him, my grandmother had had a hard life. When, after the death of my own parents at a young age, I joined Grannie in the little backstreet, my life was hard too. Hearty meals were not frequent. As a result, Mrs B's cooking was one of life's great joys to me now that I lived and worked at the third house in Derby's happily named Full Street. Mrs B never begrudged me my food and this evening was no exception. Besides I had been at the meeting at County Hall that evening. She had not. She wanted all the particulars.

"And was there really a black man on the platform, Matt?" she asked for the hundredth time, "and did he talk to the meeting?"

I nodded, my mouth too full of Mrs B's succulent and rich fruit cake to answer politely for a moment. "Yes," I said when the mouthful was properly demolished, "Mr O-*laud*-ah Equ-i-*a*-no," (I was rather proud of the way this rolled off my tongue) "Mr Olaudah Equiano, and he told us ..." I came to a sudden halt.

"Go on," she prompted eagerly, for Mrs B was a great one for news and gossip and it would increase her stock with Dr Erasmus Darwin's other servants, and those of our neighbours, if she could recount some of what this most unusual visitor to Derby had said. But all at once I felt sick and pushed away the plate of cake. The former slave's too vivid account of what he had endured had been nauseating. Quickly, I tried to shut his descriptions of the stench and festering human filth of a slave ship out of my mind but it was too late: my stomach was churning. Now the sight of food, even Mrs B's cake, became revolting.

"I can't," I groaned. "It was vile ... disgusting – I feel queasy just remembering it."

"You have gone a funny colour, Matt," she admitted. "Here! You can go outside if you're going to be sick – not in my nice clean kitchen, if you please!"

I stood up obediently to leave although the bilious feeling in my stomach was passing now. Suddenly, above the howling of the wind in the chimney a sepulchral voice spoke from the fireplace, "Cook, s-send M-Matthew to m-me; I need a w-word with him – oh, and some m-more coal in my s-s-s-s-study."

I jumped at the disembodied voice. I was still not quite used to the sudden sound of my employer speaking through his invention, a tube which communicated from his study to the kitchen. Pulling myself together I grabbed the coal scuttle which fortunately was already filled and waiting. "I'll take it, Mrs B," I said and set off for Dr Darwin's study.

I tapped on the study door and received an immediate summons to come in. The Doctor was sitting at his round writing table, his huge bulk filling and overflowing the corner chair on which he sat. He was engrossed in his writing, his right arm resting on a plump cushion for support. I took the coal scuttle over to the fireplace. The high wind had made the fire burn briskly and now all that remained was a bed of red glowing embers. I mended the fire carefully, layering on the coal with plenty of gaps. The wind sucked the smoke that rose from the new coals straight upwards and within seconds bright flames were licking at the gasses that came off the black lumps. I stood back, quietly. The Doctor's huge full-bottomed wig still bent over the slanted writing board and I waited until he sanded the paper carefully and then pushed back his overloaded chair.

"M-Matthew," he began, "the m-meeting at County Hall this evening about the p-petition to p-parliament for the abolition of the s-slave t-trade, was it well attended?"

"O yes, indeed, Sir," I replied eagerly. "Mr Strutt was in the chair, Mr Evans seconded the motion and the Hall was packed to the doors."

"D-did you g-get it all d-down in shorthand?"

"Yes, Sir," I replied proudly for I had mastered his system for note-taking completely. "I have it here," and I reached into my pocket for the neatly folded paper.

"Excellent!" he replied, "I was d-disappointed n-not to get b-back from my call to poor Mr B-Boothby in t-time but he is my p-patient – and you have the n-notes so no harm is d-done." He ran his eye over the pages I had given him. "Excellent," he repeated. "B-but now you m-must take c-care, M-Matthew. T-too m-much p-proficiency in short-hand can ruin your s-spelling in l-long-hand if you are n-not c-careful." He continued to read the paper rapidly. "Ah, g-good," he said warmly. "W-Ward from the *D-Derby M-Mercury* also addressed the m-meeting. He will g-go f-far that young m-man." Then with an abrupt change of subject he continued, "N-now, M-Matthew, the d-dispensary t-tomorrow: Dr B-Berridge will be t-taking m-my p-place. He w-will be d-doing sm-mallpox in-noculations f-free of charge and I want you t-to ..."

I listened carefully to my instructions. I felt important working at the dispensary where Derby's sick and poor could get prescriptions and advice for free: it gave me a certain standing in the town.

Having once numbered among Derby's poor myself, I knew exactly how valuable the dispensary was. And for the same reason I craved any sort of standing in Derby. For I was bent on bettering myself. My friend William Ward, of whom the Doctor had just so warmly approved, had risen from poverty himself to the respected position of newspaper editor at the precocious age of eighteen. Young as I was, I was keen to imitate him in my chosen field.

The *Derby Mercury,* of which Will was editor, was owned by the printer, Mr Drury. He had been anxious, when he first promoted Will to the post of editor, about Will's rather radical articles, for under Will's editorship the *Mercury* ran an anti-slavery piece in almost every issue, sometimes with details as gruesome as those that had made me feel so sick that evening. Far from driving readers away, however, the *Mercury's* circulation had soared under Will's hand. Any misgivings Mr Drury might have had about his readers' appetite for drinking in abolitionist propaganda with their morning tea were allayed.

Will was fearless in pursuit of the abolitionist cause and indeed of any other good cause that came his way. He did not care where that often dangerous pursuit led him and he dragged me with him whether I wanted or no. Will attended the little Particular Baptist chapel in the town and like me they must have wondered what to do with him at times. But no one with a kind heart or a love for his fellow man could help admiring Will Ward. No wonder the Baptists kept on welcoming him, for they were kindly people themselves, though more cautious than Will: he would charge into any good cause without worrying about where it would lead or who might be charging with him. But the *Mercury* did well with Will at the helm so Mr Drury gave him a free hand. In the end this led to the most monumental trouble for one newspaper though not for the *Mercury* – but I'm running ahead of myself.

Nowadays, if you walk down Agard Street, you cannot fail to notice the Baptist chapel. But at this date the building was half finished and draughty. The low benches, acquired from some former schoolroom, were unyielding and the chapel was almost bare of other furniture. But that didn't matter to us. We were young in any case. The older members must have found the benches uncomfortable but I don't remember ever hearing anyone complain. Mr Archer, the dignified banker, was generally the preacher so he just stood up – which was just as well. With his long legs, if he sat on one of the benches, his knees would have bumped his chin. And our singing had kept us warm, too, that past winter.

It was mainly for the singing that I had attached myself to the Particular Baptists (I considered their ideas rather narrow) – and my friendship with the up and coming Will, of course. Do you know *Rippon's Selection?* It was a brand new hymn book in those days. Fortified with the brief résumé of how to read musical notation that is printed just inside the front cover, we sang with a gusto that was the envy of every other non-conformist chapel in Derby. No mumbling, quavering, chilly stuff for us! There might have been higher intellectual standards and more up-to-date preaching to be found at Derby's other Dissenting chapels, especially Friargate, but they could not sing half as well as the Agard Street congregation! Three or even four real parts – we would have raised the roof if there had been much of a roof to raise. "How Firm a Foundation, Ye Saints of the Lord," you should have heard us! I know for a fact that on the particular evening I'm going to tell you about there were several people standing outside just to listen to us – which makes what happened that evening all the more strange.

It was not long after Olaudah Equiano's visit and we were at the prayer meeting. The chapel was quite crowded but one bench at the back was still empty. A big flat basket of provisions stood on it. One of the farmers' wives had brought it to quietly distribute the contents to some of the poorer members after the service. I distinctly remember walking past it and smelling the scent of new bread and a bunch of daffodils mingled with a slight whiff of Derby cheese. It brought back childhood memories. The timely arrival of exactly the same kind of generous baskets had kept Grannie and me from painful hunger not so many years ago. I settled down on my corner of the bench next to Will, waiting for Mr Archer. The memory stirred by sight of the basket served to strengthen my determination never again to be in such dire need if I could help it.

Mr Archer was a successful banker but he was no idler. Sometimes when it came to the week-night prayer meeting you could tell he was exhausted. Often he came straight from his ledgers and account-books to the service without even time for a meal. But on this dark, dreary evening there was not a trace of weariness about him: he was agog, that's the only way to describe it, with the news he had just had from Northampton.

"Four hundred million of our fellow men throughout the world in a state of pagan darkness!" he agonised. "All perishing! What pains and expense does it not deserve to rescue at least some out of so many millions from ruin! And now, at last, we can all help to do something about it." And he actually waved the paper that he had in his hand. In the light of the oil lamp by the improvised pulpit I could see he was beaming with joy. "In Northampton this very week, there has been an association meeting. Mr Ryland, Mr Hogg, Mr Fuller, Mr Sutcliffe," these were the leading ministers of the denomination, "they have founded a society called," he glanced down at the paper, "called The Particular Baptist Society for Propagating the Gospel Among the Heathen."

I knew that the idea for such a society had been discussed and discussed and discussed. I also knew that Mr Archer had been frustrated that it never got any further than discussion. But now a real, solid step had been taken: no wonder he was so delighted.

Will, keen on societies of all sorts, leaned forward on our rickety bench to listen – here was something that might go in the *Mercury*. Mr Archer went on, "Do we really believe the gospel? And yet we are prepared to allow the greater part of the world to remain in ignorance! Surely, if we ourselves have known the healing power of the gospel, if we know the Saviour, we should long for Him to be *universally* known."

"If we know the Saviour ..." Phrases like that – and there were quite a few of them when Mr Archer was preaching – always gave me an odd feeling. What did it mean, this "know the Saviour"? Was there was a hole in my experience; something those around me had that I did not have, perhaps? I looked round the chapel at the mix of people in the congregation. There was scarcely a stratum of Derby society that was unrepresented, from threadbare silk weaver to prosperous banker. No, I dismissed the thought. Surely it was just some sort of expression, a shorthand figure that indicated all the various qualities of someone who went to chapel as I did.

Will was scribbling away now; he was as fast at shorthand as I and eager to get the details right for the newspaper. Mr

Archer's words began to appear on Will's paper in a steady stream, "The soul of a Hindu or an African is surely *the same as mine* – capable of enjoying God's favour and love, capable of communing with Him, glorifying Him, and being happy in His smile for ever! How then can I ignore him?" That would go down well with the *Mercury's* abolitionist readers.

There was absolute silence in the motley congregation as we listened engrossed. In fact, it was this silence which made me almost sure that I heard something – like a sigh – at the back of the chapel. But if I had heard anything it passed from my mind as Mr Archer went on to explain what the Society proposed to do and how even we at the chapel could all help. Volunteers were to be sought who would become missionaries. The Society would raise money to send them to wherever on earth it was thought that there was most need and to provide for them while they were out there. "If God has blessed us with much earthly substance, let us offer free-heartedly to the Lord what is in reality His," entreated Mr Archer earnestly.

I looked round again as he spoke. The more shabby among us did not have much "earthly substance". They were probably wondering how they were going to help if subscriptions were needed. Dr Darwin was a kind employer but my wages were almost non-existent. It did not normally concern me that not much in the way of actual cash came my way. I was learning from the doctor all the time and it was not just practical medical learning that he provided. His researches were much more profound than mere everyday medicine. His interest in natural philosophy – science – had led him to conclusions about the very nature and origins of life itself which were deeply interesting. For anyone as keen as I was to get on in the world in the future, they were worth getting to grips with. But sometimes it frustrated me to realise that saving for a university medical training was always beyond my grasp. There was certainly not much "earthly substance" available and nor would I have wanted to contribute it to the missionary cause if I had had any. No, I'm afraid it would have gone straight into the Matthew Batchelor advancement fund! I was as glad therefore as the most destitute member to hear Mr Archer continue, "and whether we can or cannot honour the Lord in this with our substance let us attend the generous donations of those that are able to contribute to the support of His cause with our most fervent prayers."

And with that the chapel members really did get down to it. They were as fervent in prayer as they were in singing and the better-off members were just as heartfelt as the poorer ones in their earnest prayers for the new Society. As I listened it was clear that, in pounds and in prayers, Agard Street in general would be more forthcoming than Matthew Batchelor in particular.

Towards the end of the meeting I thought I heard that strange sigh again – or was it just someone whispering a low "Amen" to old brother James's plea that God would provide missionaries for the Society to send even from among those gathered at Agard Street?

We finished by singing Thomas Gibbon's "Father, is not Thy promise pledged" which ends with two rousing verses exactly to the point:

From east to west from south to north
Now be His name adored!
Europe with all thy millions shout
Hosannas to thy Lord.

Asia and Africa resound
From shore to shore His fame
And thou America in songs
Redeeming love proclaim!

We could be heard right across Derby!

The meeting was over. Farmer Brown's wife slipped to the back to collect her basket of good things before her less well-off neighbours went out into the chill March wind. I turned to Will, who was energetically putting the finishing touches to his notes, "... concluded in singing the well known hymn that ends with the lines, *Asia and Africa ...*"

A piercing scream came from the back of the chapel and the farmer's wife crumpled up in a faint.

Chapter two

SCIPIO AFRICANUS

1792

So wings the wounded Deer her headlong flight,
Pierced by some ambush'd archer of the night ...

(Erasmus Darwin: The Botanic Garden. Part II.)

*W*hen I reached the back of the chapel the scene was chaotic but Mrs Brown, now sitting trembling on a bench, her basket overturned and her bonnet dishevelled, was not receiving much attention. For beside her, lying half under a nearby bench was a huge man, half naked, with blood crusted on, and oozing from, wounds on his back. That alone would have been electrifying enough. But I hardly noticed these appalling details. The only thing I saw at that instant was that the man was black – deep, dark, shining, ebony black.

Mr Archer, used to wielding authority, took charge of the situation. "Stand back everyone, please. Thank you, thank you. Sarah, can you assist Mrs Brown to move out of the way?" He took me by the arm, "Matthew, would you present my compliments to Doctor Darwin, please, and ask if we could trouble him to step over – in a medical capacity – for a moment?"

I needed no second bidding and sped off back to Full Street at once, knowing that the Doctor would be interested in this extraordinary turn of events in any capacity, medical or otherwise.

Mr Archer may have been tall but Dr Darwin's massive bulk towered over him. "A s-surgeon will be needed t-to d-dress these wounds," he said when he had finished his examination. "I would s-suggest you s-send for Mr F-Fox or Mr L-Ley. If you mention that it is at m-my request and explain the c-circumstances, I have n-no d-doubt one of them w-would be w-willing to c-come out and attend on him. The p-patient is extremely chilled and should be given b-brandy and w-warmth. You will n-need to f-find out where he has c-come from in d-due c-course b-but n-not on any account should he b-be t-troubled with questions at the m-moment."

Questions! I wondered if the man even spoke English until I remembered Mr Olaudah Equiano. The doctor continued, "He has lost s-sufficient b-blood that I should n-not recommend b-bleeding him." Then he turned to me and added, "Remain here, M-Matthew, and then when the p-patient has been accommodated come b-back and let me have the d-details."

It was exceptionally late that evening when I returned to Full Street to make my report to the Doctor, but when I did I was fairly bursting with the news.

"Farmer Brown and his wife took him home with them when Mr Ley the surgeon had finished," I said in answer to his questions about the wounded stranger's present whereabouts, "but he was already much better when we got him into the chapel house next door. Once he was by the kitchen fire and had a dribble of brandy inside him and the chapel keeper had found him a blanket, he really revived. Before Mr Ley arrived he was talking – just in a low whisper – but I reminded Mr Archer of what you had said, Sir, about not questioning him, and after that, what with the pain of having his wounds dressed as well, we kept him quiet."

"G-good," said the Doctor, pushing aside his writing board and turning to face me, "and w-what d-did he m-manage to tell you b-before the s-surgeon arrived?"

"He is a runaway," I replied, "an indentured servant, I suppose, (since he cannot be a slave here in England can he?) of a Mr Herrod of Nottingham."

"Whether he is a s-slave or a s-servant is an interesting p-point," the Doctor replied."It was by no m-means clearly established by the S-Somerset legal case in 'seventy-two that a s-slave is free when he s-sets foot in England – although that is the p-popular understanding. But did he t-tell you his n-name?"

"Yes, Sir," I answered. "He is called Africanus, Sir, Scipio Africanus."

"The n-name of the ancient Roman General who c-conquered C-Carthage in N-North Africa," said the Doctor. "S-some m-master has g-given him that n-name either through ignorance of its full s-significance or to shame an African by n-naming him after one who c-conquered a g-great c-city of his ancestors."

Farmer and Mrs Brown were a prosperous old couple. It was typical of them to volunteer to take home an injured slave and care for him without any questions about who he was or what he might have done. They had the farm cart with them – Farmer Brown had been delivering something or other in Derby that evening – so why not take the wounded stranger back with them to the farm at Mackworth to look after? The Browns were quietly open-handed people. Their generosity had often eased hard times among Derby's silk workers and china makers. They were loved as a result in Derby's less prosperous back streets. A runaway slave? They were as keen on abolition as Will Ward himself and glad to be able to do something solid and practical to help.

As soon as I was finished at the dispensary the next day I took myself off (with the Doctor's full permission) to Mackworth. Will Ward was also desperate to come but he could not leave the print-shop: the *Mercury* must be out the next day. The spring sunshine was pleasant after the rain and the banks of the lanes were dotted with primroses. I covered the short distance in no time.

Mrs Brown's capable little kitchen maid, Susan, was all smiles as she welcomed me to her domain. "Oh, you should see him, Mr Batchelor," she said, "he is so tall and gracious, every bit a gentleman – and such talk! Why I could listen to him all day! Mr Africanus," she added as she opened the door, "a visitor for you. Mr Matthew Batchelor from the dispensary – and if you'll excuse me, Sirs, I'm needed in the dairy now."

Scipio Africanus was sitting by the kitchen fire. Dressed in breeches and a fustian jacket that Mrs Brown had dug out from somewhere and which were just a little too tight for him, he carefully removed a rug from his knees before standing up to greet me. I held out my hand.

"Mr Batchelor," he said and, to my surprise, his voice was deep and rich with all the inflections of cultured and cultivated English, "I owe you many thanks," and he took my hand and shook it warmly. Now that I was close to him I could see that he was not much older than myself, despite his imposing physical appearance.

"I am glad I could help," I said a little awkwardly. "May I ask how you came to be in the chapel?"

Scipio Africanus smiled. "I had swum across the river and was trying to make my way across the city under cover of darkness," he said. "I was becoming weary with cold and loss of blood when I heard you singing. It was a hymn of which my poor mistress had been very fond. I felt sure God was leading me to those who would shelter me."

I was staggered. "You swam the Derwent – in that state!" I exclaimed. The Derwent is a deep, cold, fast-flowing river with dangerous currents to say nothing of the weirs. To swim across it was a feat enough without a wounded, bleeding back! Doctor Darwin owned a shady apple orchard on the opposite bank of the river which flowed at the bottom of his garden in Full Street. He had rigged up a sort of chain-ferry boat so that his children could cross the Derwent to the orchard. But they were strictly forbidden to swim in the river. Then the rest of my new friend's remarks struck me and I asked, "You are a Christian then – I mean – that is – you sing hymns and ..."

"I am an African and a Christian," he replied, gently dignified. "Does that surprise you?"

Suddenly I felt ashamed. Why should he not be?

He noticed my confusion and said kindly, "Would you care to hear my story? If you did, I think you would understand."

"I would be most gratified," I said precisely, for his own careful language prompted a similar style in my own.

"I was taken from Africa to Jamaica to be a slave as a tiny child," he began. "I do not remember anything of this except a cold feeling that grips my heart when I try to think of the time before I entered Mrs Herrod's house. Nor do I remember my mother. My earliest memory is of gentle Mrs Herrod who trained me up to be her servant, teaching me to read, to speak correctly, to cipher and above all to know the Lord."

Again that familiar yet puzzling phrase. But I could not pause to consider it for Scipio was continuing his fascinating account. "With Mr Herrod I had little to do, although I understand that he gave me my name. He is a cruel and bitter man with a heart of iron. From Jamaica I removed with my mistress and her husband here to England. She kindly told me that it had been resolved many years ago in Parliament that England has too pure an air for slaves to breathe in and that I was therefore a free man. She gave me indentures for seven years since I wished to continue her servant but, not long afterwards, she died.

"I was now at the mercy of Mr Herrod who made use of the skill I had learned in keeping accounts. It was not long before, having fallen on hard times, he decided to return to Jamaica, taking me with him for I was useful to him in his business. I told him I was a free man, though I had been indentured to his late wife, and I did not wish to return to Jamaica. I knew, if I did, I would be enslaved again. He replied that that was none of my business and he would compel me to accompany him. He forced me to go with him on his journey towards Liverpool, coming first to Derby where he had business. Arriving at the house of a friend whose character was like his own on the other side of the river, he first whipped me and then locked me up – as he thought – before settling down to carouse with his companion. But he had made a poor job of fastening the lock and I was able to open the door and escape.

"I thought my only hope was to enter the town and try to find someone, some officer of the law or perhaps someone at some chapel or even at the office of the newspaper, to help me, for I was not ignorant of the efforts of good men in England to end the trade in slaves and indeed slavery itself in Jamaica. I had heard too of the legal case that made taking Africans such as me back to slavery in Jamaica illegal. I swam the river but, although the darkness aided me, I had no means of finding my way and I was now terribly cold. Then in God's good providence, I heard you all singing and praising God. I crawled in – for by this time I could no longer stand – and thought to hide under a bench until the service was over, for I was not suitably clad for attending a service of worship. Alas, my strength was spent. I tried to listen to the good words being spoken but my eyes closed and I seemed to slip away."

At this point Susan appeared again looking flustered to announce, "Mr Ward of the *Mercury*, Sirs," and in walked Will, all bursting to make Scipio Africanus's further acquaintance. He had been sent on this congenial errand by Mr Drury himself. Scipio had to go over his experiences again for Will's benefit. When he had finished, Will exclaimed, "Illegal! I should think it is! The Somerset Case in 'seventy-two: '... no master ever was allowed here to take a slave by force to be sold abroad ...' – you are a free man, Scipio Africanus! And," he added, "if you want work in Derby when you are feeling better, I am pretty sure Mr Drury at the *Mercury* could find you a position. He was about to advertise for a man with a head for figures to work in the shop and I have a feeling you would be just what he needs!"

Chapter three

MARKET HEAD

1792

Now, happier lot! enlighten'd realms possess
The learned labours of the immortal Press;
Nursed on whose lap the births of science thrive,
And rising Arts the wrecks of Time survive.

*(Erasmus Darwin, The Temple of Nature;
or, The Origin of Society)*

*W*illiam Ward was as good as his word. A mild, sunny April saw Scipio restored to health and established in the little shop on the ground floor of Drury's printers at Market Head. It was just visible from Full Street even in the evening by the mellow glow of Derby's street lamps. Here he oversaw the sale not only of books and newspapers but herbal medicines and apothecaries' preparations.

I grew to like Scipio immensely. His formal language and manner of address, his polished speech, never seemed to falter. From the first time I met him it had prompted as similar tone in me. As I spent more time with him my own manner of speech gradually improved under his influence and I lost the remnants of my broad Derby vowels. My respect for his cultured voice also deepened into a regard for his whole thoughtful, warm and dignified personality. That wonderful voice and his unique African appearance made him a popular feature of Drury's shop too. I think sales rose as a direct result. It seemed totally natural for Will and me to admit him into our friendship and it was just as well we did for Will's next clash with the authorities was to have serious consequences. Will was going to need all the support he could get.

I called in at the *Mercury* offices late one afternoon, as spring was merging into summer. I had finished work at the dispensary and I carried with me a note from Dr Darwin giving Will information about a meeting of the Derby Society for Political Information. If I had thought about it at the time, I would have realised that Will's deepening involvement in this society, of which I too, I admit, was a member, spelled real trouble.

The Derby Society for Political Information had been founded by Dr Darwin and his friends as a kind of talking-shop for those with radical ideas; the sort of ideas that were very unpopular with the government – and very popular with William Ward. They appealed to me also but for different – and personal – reasons. I could work until I became an apothecary but I would never be granted the respect given to a doctor, however much I learned. The radicals, such as those who were members of the Derby Society, attacked the attitudes, the blocks on advancement, that I considered held back someone like me. Radicalism therefore appealed to me.

Yet I was wary: the English radicals admired revolutionary France where the idea that all men were equal was being pressed to its logical conclusion. I knew well that too warm an espousal of such ideas on my part, should it become known, would probably block the very advancement I craved, however hard I worked. Those in power consider ideas that threaten their means of control dangerous. Even in free England you had to be careful. Not only must you work hard, you must keep out of trouble too. I was therefore more cautious than the reckless Will, who seemed to thrive on dangerous ideas.

The bookshop was shut for the night when I arrived and Scipio was engaged in casting up the day's accounts for Mr Drury. Will had just seen the latest edition of the *Mercury* through the press and was in high spirits. We were all together, squeezed into the stuffy little box of a basement room where Scipio kept his ledgers. Through the tiny window near the ceiling came the sounds of the market people dispersing, hand carts trundling past on squeaky wheels and the weary homeward tramp of feet. Then even that breath of fresh air was denied us for Will had news to share that was not to be overheard by casual passers-by. He reached up and pulled the window shut. At once the trundling and tramping died away.

"I got a letter from old Yorke today," he said in triumph. "No idea how he got it through but it was pushed under the door – Scipio found it when he unlocked the shop this morning. I held the *Mercury* back to put in some of Yorke's information – direct from Paris! We don't need to rely on repeating what is in the London papers here at the *Derby Mercury;* we have our own agent at the heart of French affairs, good old Redhead Yorke. We get inside information!"

"And an exhilarating style of prose as well," I added, laughing, "if Redhead's letters are anything like his oratory! What's been happening then?" I was as eager as anyone in those heady days for news from revolutionary France, despite my caution. Like Will, and many others, I was sure the French would benefit as thcy thiew off the yoke of their oppressive government and persecuting church. They should look across the Channel, I thought. For all its faults, England had an altogether more free society that would provide an example of good government to the newly liberated French. Some French revolutionaries, of course, were for going much further than the English model. I suspended my judgment as to whether we English should return the compliment and look to the French example as some Radicals advocated. They were already agitating for votes for all men, new parliamentary elections every single year and so on.

William Ward thought these were good ideas and they were energetically preached by his friend, Redhead Yorke.

"The French are still trying to follow the example we set in our own Revolution of 1688," Will replied to my request for news. "A few days ago a huge demonstration took place in Paris, Redhead says. They wanted to persuade the king to lay down his power of veto over the proceedings of their National Assembly. Their representative talked of being ready to resist oppression according to their Declaration of the *Rights of Man ...*"

"Did they succeed?" I asked, glancing involuntarily up at the fastened window. "What does Redhead say?"

"He says," said Will whipping a bundle of papers out of his pocket and thumbing through them, "he says ... yes here it is ... *Journée du 20 juin ...* 20th of June twenty thousand *sans-culottes* were on the march first to the National Assembly and then to the Royal Palace. They were peaceful, offering no violence although they were armed. The Assembly, after deliberation, allowed them to cross its hall, rank on rank singing their revolutionary anthem and said it would take their petition into consideration. Then the *sans-culottes* went to the palace. The king commanded the outer doors of the palace to be opened and they streamed in. They began forcing open the inner doors with hatchets but the king commanded them to be opened for them and appeared himself with the National Guard securing his person. The king delighted them by putting on one of their red caps of liberty which someone offered to him on the top of a pike ..."

The temperature rose in the little room. Scipio looked up from his ledgers. "Are you carrying that letter around with you, Will?" he asked. "If I were you, I would lock it up in that, er, *private* compartment that Mr Drury has at the back of the desk in his office. You could end up before the magistrate as an agitator otherwise. A letter such as that from Paris – and from a radical like Redhead Yorke – in your very pocket would be enough evidence if it were to be found."

It was an accurate observation. The Prime Minister, Pitt, was concerned about revolutionary ideas reaching Britain from France. Radicals were being watched and Will's articles in the *Mercury* definitely put him in the radical category. If just one of the hands in the print shop decided to earn extra money by becoming a government spy, Will's every movement would be reported. I looked up at the closed window again and suddenly felt as though I were stifling.

Will sighed. "The French have suffered generations of unjust government," he said. "The common people have had to bear all the taxes needed to pay for long wars and the great luxury and extravagance of the court. In spite of this, they themselves have been unable to have any say in the government of the country because their parliament is useless to them, yet ..."

"Why useless?" I interrupted.

"Because it has not met since 1614!" Will replied.

"1614!" I gasped, "that's over a hundred and seventy years. And we complain because we don't have parliamentary elections annually!"

"Yes, and who paid all the taxes in France meanwhile? The poor peasants: it took most of their earnings. And it was wasted mostly because the tax collection system was so chaotic and corrupt. But, *of course,*" there was a note of sarcasm in his voice here, "the nobles and clergy were exempt from taxation completely. Then there were famines, brutal treatment of peasants by landlords ..."

"No wonder they want something better!"

"If they can only get freedom, as we did in 1688, without loss of blood ... I never advocate violence in the *Mercury* – I hope you've noticed, Matt, how careful I am," Will added, "- always peaceful means of reform and so on, yet here I am having to lock up my letters!"

"Speaking of letters, I've got a note for you from Dr Darwin," I said, remembering my errand. "He wanted to notify you of the next meeting of the Political Information Society, 16th July I think, at the Talbot just up the road," and I passed him the note.

Will unfolded the note and glanced at it, then he started reading away in earnest. It was a longer message than I had expected.

"Well, look at this!" he exclaimed when he had finished. "The Doctor does not just want me to go to the meeting; he wants me to address it! I'm to write a Declaration summarising our objectives, and introduce it to the meeting in a form suitable for printing and circulating to other Political and Corresponding Societies. He's even noted down some of the points he wants me to cover here."

Scipio looked up from his ledgers again and mopped his face with a spotless linen handkerchief. He was uneasy.

"There's a complete assortment of people in that society," I said. "The Strutts from Friargate Chapel, Mr Fox, Dr Crompton, all respectable people but the subscriptions are deliberately low so that poor people, our own English *sans-culottes* if you like, can join too. There are bound to be plenty of them at the meeting. How will you get the point over so that everyone understands ...?"

"I'll re-emphasise that the aim is to have no violent intentions," said Will, "and make sure that they understand that levelling – redistributing the wealth of the rich to the poor – is not what we are aiming at; we *only* want fair representation in government."

Scipio's pen began scratching away at the ledgers again and his handkerchief was returned to his pocket.

"Make sure you distance yourself from the extreme French revolutionaries who want to sweep everything away violently, you mean?" I asked.

"Exactly," replied Will, "and I'll be careful too; there are people at Friargate that have, well, theological views that don't go down well in the poorer parts of town."

Scipio looked up again, "You mean they do not believe in the Trinity or the divinity of Christ," he said flatly. "That is why the people, the English *sans-culottes* you called them, Matt, burnt down dissenters' chapels and Mr Priestley's house and rioted for three days in Birmingham last year."

Will seemed surprised at this blunt remark from the usually quiet and gracious Scipio and for a moment he was silent. "Well, yes," he said at last, "but Mr Priestley's theological views weren't the only reason for the riots, you know. I just mean I must make sure they understand that all varieties of beliefs are represented by this Declaration not just those at the chapel in Friargate."

"The working people are not nice, not exact, in their distinctions," said Scipio. "In Birmingham any dissenter was deemed unorthodox and therefore of the same beliefs as Mr Priestley as far as they were concerned. They considered *all* chapels as places where heresy is taught."

"The Trinity *is* a difficult doctrine to understand," I said airily, "How can God be God the Father and Jesus Christ be the God the Son and yet there be only one God – to say nothing of the Holy Spirit – I'm sure I can't fathom it. To be honest, I can't quite see why people make such a fuss."

Scipio opened his mouth to answer when Will said, "Why don't you ask Dr Darwin, Matt? He's a churchman isn't he?"

"I suppose so," I answered, wondering if he really was even as I spoke. "He doesn't exactly go to church often ..."

"A good many churchmen don't," laughed Will. "They are not all like good old Wilberforce at Clapham! Now I'm sure he never misses."

William Wilberforce, MP for Yorkshire, though some ten years Will's senior, was certainly not "old" but he was indeed good. He was both Will's and Scipio's hero in the campaign for the abolition of slavery and he worked relentlessly as an MP in parliament for that cause. With radical reforms such as those proposed by the Redhead Yorks of the political world, however, Wilberforce would have nothing to do.

Will went off to Mr Drury's office to hide away his dangerous French dispatch in the heavy old desk. Scipio opened the window and the sweet fresh air blew in again and with it now a peaceful quiet. The last market stallholders had gone home and the street was deserted.

The massive oak desk with its secret drawer had been at the printers' since Mr Drury took over the business from his uncle but, strange to say, it had come from my own family originally. I never thought about it without a tinge of sadness. My own grandmother had sold it, along with most of her other furniture, when she fell on hard times – hard times that were closely connected with the desk itself and with the drawer. I must have sighed at the thought because Scipio looked up.

"Will told me an interesting story about Mr Drury's desk," he said.

"Did he?"

"Yes, but he could not remember the full details. It was your grandmother's, was it not, and all her valuables were stolen from that secret drawer?"

I nodded. "Long before my time," I said, "in 1745."

"How did it happen?" he asked.

"To start with you have to understand about the two pretenders," I began, "Charles Edward Stuart, the Young Pretender and his father James Francis Edward Stuart, the Old Pretender. Both of them were descendants of King James II."

"Pretender?" queried Scipio.

"Yes, pretender to the throne. You see their forebear, James II, had lost the throne and the Young Pretender was trying to get it back on behalf of the Old Pretender. He went to Scotland first and then came here with his followers. They wanted to push King George II off the throne and bring in the Old Pretender instead."

"They came to Derby?"

"Yes, and everyone was terrified in case there was fighting."

"What did they do then, the people of Derby?"

"When they heard the Young Pretender was on his way to Derby," I explained, "anyone who had valuables hid them (it was too dangerous to carry more than a small amount with them) and then hurried off elsewhere to safety. My grandfather put all his gold and my grandmother's jewellery into the secret drawer, locked the house and took her and my father, who was only a baby, away to safety."

"But," said Scipio, "when he returned ..."

"He never did return," I said. "The Young Pretender got no further than Derby on his journey to London. He turned round here and began to make his way back towards Scotland and defeat. But before my grandfather could make his own return, I'm sorry to say he met with an accident, fell from his horse and was killed. He was not a particularly good horseman and I think he was exhausted by the circumstances. It was dark ... I'm not really sure what happened exactly."

"Alas!" sympathised Scipio, "your poor grandmother!"

"Yes," I said, "and there was more to come. When she returned home she found that, like some others, her house had been broken into. The secret desk drawer was open and all the valuables gone. Whoever it was who had made off with her wealth was never found and she herself grew gradually poorer and poorer."

"What did she do?" asked Scipio. "Did she not have a family to support her?"

"When my father grew up I believe she was a little better off for a while," I said, "but both my parents died when I was still only small. Before I was old enough to help support us both, all her furniture except a few poor belongings had been sold and we were living in one room in a mean house in Derby's backstreets. Not long after I found work with Dr Darwin and could help her with what little I earned, she died, leaving me alone in the world."

Scipio tutted sympathetically as he let me out of the print shop into the dusk of the empty street.

"No news of Mr Herrod, Scipio?" I asked, for I was keen not to go on reliving these dark memories. We had all three been concerned about what might happen if his former bully of a master should turn up and try to claim him.

"No, I'm thankful to say, Matt," he replied.

"That's good news," I said. "By now he must have continued on his journey to Jamaica, resigned to losing you after all."

"I truly hope so, Matt," he said, "and I hope Dr Darwin has a good answer to your question."

"My question?" Talk of the old desk and all it stood for had driven our earlier discussion from my mind. "Oh, yes, that. Goodnight, Scipio."

As I made my way back to Full Street, I wondered if in reality Scipio himself might be more qualified than Dr Darwin to comment on such a topic. I knew that he would say that he "knew the Saviour", whatever that meant, and he believed in the Trinity, whatever it was. I was much less sure about the Doctor's position.

A few days later I was in Dr Darwin's study working at the writing desk. The Doctor was not just a medical man, although he tended to keep quiet about his other activities for fear his patients would not approve. He was sure they all wanted a physician who concentrated solely on medicine and was not distracted by other things. Nevertheless he was involved in almost every kind of scientific or engineering project that was going on at the time, from canals to carriage wheels and a founder member – if not *the* founder member – of the Birmingham Lunar Society. This was quite simply a group of the best brains in the land. They met for dinner regularly when the moon was full, the moonlight enabling them to easily see their way to ride home after dark. Though further from Birmingham now than he had been when he lived at Litchfield, the Doctor still attended the Lunar Society meetings whenever he could.

I admired the Doctor's wide-ranging mind enormously. How I would have liked to be able to be a member of the Lunar Society myself one day: the *Lunaticks* they called themselves in jest. After all, many of them were men who had risen from poor backgrounds; why should not I? Alas, I knew only too well what might stand in my way. They were mostly engineers. In my field, medicine, no one could practise as a respectable doctor without a university qualification. I could see no way to amass enough money for that.

I stared up at the strange carved wooden half-head, the working part of the Doctor's still uncompleted mechanical speaking machine, that glowered down at me from the shelf above the desk. When the Doctor was working on it, it had never got further than saying "mama" and "papa" although I suppose that was a remarkable achievement in itself. I had never, I am glad to say, heard it utter a syllable. The Doctor had also invented and constructed a copying machine with a double pen arrangement. This was completed but as it was on permanent loan to his lawyer son, any duplicates the Doctor needed of his notes or other writings had to be made by me.

I was hard at work that day copying a draft of part of the Doctor's medical book which was to be called, *Zoonomia*. My task was to make the Doctor's revisions and re-orderings of the book over some twenty years of medical practice into a finished manuscript. Painstaking care was needed to ensure that the Doctor's latest thoughts were inserted in the correct places.

Copying is an excellent way of learning. The book in its final form was to cover everything from digestion to drunkenness and I intended to learn it all. It was even going to deal with the very origin of life itself. I copied the massive sentences assiduously, clause by clause:

From thus meditating on the great similarity of the structure of the warm-blooded animals,
and at the same time of the great changes they undergo both before and after their nativity;
and by considering in how minute a portion of time many of the

changes of animals above described have been produced;
would it be too bold to imagine,
that in the great length of time,
since the earth began to exist,
perhaps millions of ages before the commencement of the history
of mankind,
would it be too bold to imagine,
that all warm-blooded animals have arisen from one living
filament,
which the GREAT FIRST CAUSE endued with animality,
with the power of acquiring new parts,
attended with new propensities,
directed by irritations, sensations, volitions, and associations;
and thus possessing the faculty of continuing to improve by
its own inherent activity,
and of delivering down those improvements by generation to its
posterity, world without end!

I was just wondering whether this vast, paragraph-length sentence should really end with a question mark rather than an exclamation mark, when the Doctor himself entered the room.

"Ah, M-Matthew," he said, as I stood up respectfully. "H-hard at work! Excellent! How f-far have you g-got now?" He leant over the desk scrutinising my work. I was glad that I had learnt a neat legible hand from my grandmother. "And how m-much of what you have c-copied do you understand?"

"Oh, I think I have grasped a great deal," I replied, "though the chapter on capillary glands and membranes I think I have not fully understood and there are things in the chapter on the liver which ..."

He motioned me to sit down. "I m-meant how m-much of what you have j-just copied," he said.

Chapter four
FIRST CAUSE
1792

Still Nature's births enclosed in egg or seed,
From the tall forest to the lowly weed,
Her beaux and beauties, butterflies and worms,
Rise from aquatic to aerial forms.

(Erasmus Darwin, The Temple of Nature)

"This chapter, Sir?" I asked, slightly surprised. "This s-sentence," he replied, pointing to what I had just copied.

I looked at it, somewhat startled. To be truthful, I had been so intent on accuracy and on the question of punctuation that had puzzled me that I had hardly had time to consider the meaning of what I had copied down: ... *that in the great length of time ... since the earth began to exist ... millions of ages before the commencement of the history of mankind ... the power of acquiring new parts ... delivering down those improvements by generation to its posterity ... world without end ... GREAT FIRST CAUSE ...* For a moment the words seemed to swim before my eyes. Then suddenly I had an inspiration.

"Well, Sir, it is odd that you mention it. I was discussing the doctrine of the Trinity with some friends earlier this week and someone suggested you would know all about it. The Great First Cause – that is it, isn't it, Sir? I mean, that is why you have put it in capitals ..."

The Doctor settled his huge form comfortably in his corner chair and smiled. "I d-don't think I can claim to be an authority on the T-Trinity," he began, "although I have a n-number of f-friends in the L-Lunar S-Society who have c-considered the question deeply and come to ... c-certain, shall we say negative, c-conclusions of their own. But I certainly agree that the n-natural world we s-see around us requires a c-cause." He paused and then went on, "You must unders-stand that the ideas to which I am ab-bout to introduce you are n-not ones which a p-prominent physician openly espouses if he w-wishes to keep his valuable p-patients. This is w-what still m-makes me hesitant about p-publishing them in b-book form, even as p-poetry." I must have looked puzzled for he continued, "In p-p-plain language, I talk ab-bout these things only to those I can t-trust, m-members of the L-Lunar S-Society, and so on, otherwise m-my m-medical p-practice m-might s-suffer."

I was deeply flattered. Here was the great Doctor trusting me with ideas he reserved for his anonymously published poems – and his friends in the Lunar Society. I drank in his words as he explained his discoveries. I became so absorbed in what he was saying that I no longer noticed his stammer.

"The existence of a first cause, you can call him 'God' for convenience if you wish, can be demonstrated by mathematics. This is the Great Architect, the Cause of Causes, the Parent of Parents that formed this world. Nor is it any disparagement of the Deity to consider that he created living beings not in an instant but by a certain process of cause and effect. For, if we can do such a thing as compare one infinity with another, it would seem to require a greater infinity of power to cause the causes of effects, than to cause the effects themselves. Are you following me, Matthew?"

"Yes, Sir," I paused to digest his words. "You are saying that we do not insult God, if we consider that he made the creation we see around us by a long and gradual process rather than by speaking it into existence directly. For he must then have created the process of creation itself, which is a greater marvel."

He nodded. "Good. Now, we find by careful observation that the earth was originally covered with water, as appears from some of its highest mountains consisting of shells cemented together – the limestone rocks of the Alps, for instance. Therefore, we conclude that animal life began beneath the sea. This life, originally a single living point, fibre or filament, had the power to change. We see changes in life all around us. Caterpillars change into butterflies. Over generations animals may be bred with different features and abilities from their forebears. Or consider the tadpole, which changes into a frog! These arguments show that all vegetables and animals change and could arise from a small beginning, a filament. I am giving you now a bare outline of the *method* of creation."

I nodded again and he continued, "After islands or continents were raised above the primeval ocean, great numbers of the most simple animals would seek food at the edges of the new land. So they might gradually become amphibious; as is now seen in the frog, who changes from an aquatic animal to an amphibious one, as I have already mentioned, or in the gnat, which changes from a swimming to a flying creature."

"And people?" I asked, "Human beings?"

"The same method," he replied. "Think about the great similarity of structure, which all the warm-blooded animals, birds, amphibious animals and mankind share; from the mouse and bat to the elephant and whale. One can conclude that they have all been produced from an original living filament through small changes over millions of ages of time."

"And yet ..." I struggled for words, "and yet that is not what most people think, is it?"

"Not yet, not here in the society in which we move, no," he replied. "But in other ages and in other parts of the world, man has come to this understanding, and a few – a privileged few – in our day also understand. You, Matthew, will come to this understanding also."

Would I? Exciting visions of myself as part of the "privileged few", a member of the Lunar society, flitted across my mind. Yet I was a little perplexed. "Why have most people not grasped it here and now, then?"

"I will l-leave you to c-consider what holds them b-back, M-Matthew," he answered, and then, after a pause as if to allow me to consider his words, he went on in a more practical tone, "but for the p-present we must turn our thoughts to increasing the t-total of human h-happiness around us by less theoretical m-means: d-did you p-pass my n-note to Mr W-William W-Ward?"

"Yes, Sir, and he went at once to think out an address for the meeting," I answered.

"Good," replied the Doctor, "I will j-jot d-down one or two more s-suggestions which you can p-pass on to him," and he reached for his pen.

Monstrous creatures with vague outlines were struggling out of the water onto the shore of some sea or body of water. No sooner did they arise than they began attempting to slaughter and devour one another. The savage growls and barks of the biters and tearers mingled with the howls and groans of the bitten and torn in a cacophony of horror. Wave upon wave of monsters arose from the sea and as they did so those already on the land began to assume more definite shapes, frogs, horses, lions and last of all men, men with hideous cruel faces, with claws for hands and some with beaks or with fangs. Their growls and grunts, too, became words, indistinct at first but gradually distinguishable: "Back, back ... holds us back ..." mingled with their hideous shrieks and moans. They towered over me and I tried to flee or to cry out but I could neither move nor speak. "Back ... back ... *He* holds us back ... You must not seek to know *Him* ... *He* holds back us, *us,* the privileged few! Back ... back ... back ..." It rose in a terrible chant. With a tremendous struggle I managed to kick out at the monsters and I woke to find that my efforts had jolted the coverlet from my narrow bed. I was bathed in chilly perspiration. Through the window of my attic room, a blaze of cold stars almost dazzled me in the clear night sky. I shuddered, picked up the coverlet and drifted back into a troubled sleep.

Chapter five

THE TALBOT INN ADDRESS

1792-3

So now, where Derwent rolls his dusky floods,
Through vaulted mountains, and a night of woods, ...
His ponderous oars to slender spindles turns,
And pours o'er massy wheels his foamy urns, ...
With wiry teeth *revolving cards* release,
The tangled knots, and smooth the ravell'd fleece;
Next moves the *iron-hand* with fingers fine,
Combs the wide card, and forms the eternal line;
Slow, with soft lips, the *whirling Can* acquires,
The tender skeins, and wraps in rising spires;
With quicken'd pace *successive rollers* move,

And these retain, and those extend the rove;
Then fly the spoles, the rapid axles glow; –
And slowly circumvolves the labouring wheel below.

(Erasmus Darwin The Botanic Garden. Part II.)

———————

*W*ill spent a great deal of time and trouble composing his address, recognising how important it might be. He rehearsed the results of his deliberations to Scipio and me whenever he had a chance. He had a particular hero among those who were involved in the revolution in France, a Protestant pastor named Jean-Paul Rabaut Saint-Étienne. This Monsieur Rabaut was conspicuous for standing up for the freedom of French Protestants to worship and to live their lives without harassment as well as for more general freedoms. Will was inclined to model himself on the French pastor's pattern. When Drury's bookshop got hold of copies of Pastor Rabaut's chronicle of the events of the revolution, Will was ecstatic.

The rain was driving down outside (it was one of the wettest summers anyone could remember) but Will's enthusiasm was not dampened. "Look what I've got!" he enthused, clutching a stock copy, "by that Monsieur Rabaut I told you about. He is a member of the French National Assembly now. His history of the French Revolution has just come out in English and here it is! It is sure to be popular. Scipio, you've sold dozens of copies in the bookshop already, haven't you? Listen to this! I'm going to put it in the 'address.'" He raised his hand as though holding forth to a crowd and began:

"'We, who are only the people, but who pay for wars with our substance and our blood, will not cease to tell Kings, or Governments, that to them alone wars are profitable: that the true and just conquests are those which each makes at home, by comforting the peasantry, by promoting agriculture and manufacturing: by multiplying men, and the other productions of nature; that then it is that Kings may call themselves the image of God ... If they continue to make us fight and kill one another in uniform, we will continue to write and speak, until nations shall be cured of this folly.'"

Will was a wonderful reader and he brought the words to life with great drama. But Scipio had been scanning the content, rather than the manner of delivery. "In uniform!" He picked up the word. "You need to be careful, Will. England is on the verge of war with France. You will be thought to be urging the soldiers and sailors to mutiny if you quote a Frenchman (even a Protestant) who talks of those *in uniform* not being forced to fight against their will."

Will was unabashed. "That's not what I'm saying ... not exactly ..." he said. Then moving on quickly as though to dismiss Scipio's objection, "And I've tried to get across that our own methods are peaceful, not rioting and so on. Look, I'll try the introduction out on you. What do you think?" And he set off again declaiming with gusto: "We are in the pursuit of truth, in a peaceable, calm, and unbiased manner; and wherever we recognize her features, we will embrace her as the companion of happiness, of wisdom, and of peace. This is the mode of our conduct: the reasons for it will be found in the following declaration of our opinions, to the whole of which each member gives his hearty assent ..."

We listened in silence to Will's rhetoric. I could tell Scipio was uneasy. He scratched his nose and looked down at the floor, especially when Will got on to the address itself. Then Will started talking about taxes and the poor having no representatives to ensure their tax money was not, as he put it, "improperly and wickedly spent."

Scipio raised his head and said, "You owe too much to Tom Paine's book, Will," meaning *Rights of Man* by Paine which was very popular with those who wanted to see parliamentary reform and very *un*popular with the government, "and I think your language is ungracious. Paine is no friend of Christianity – not of Christianity as revealed in the Bible at any rate."

"Nothing will be done towards liberty if we do not speak plainly," said Will, ignoring the last part of Scipio's remark, "and Paine speaks plainly."

"I am a friend of liberty," said Scipio, quietly, "for I know what it means to have none. But I do not like republicanism or such bitter speech."

I knew that Will was a real enthusiast for the *Rights of Man*. It was circulating at all levels of society in cheap editions as well as expensive ones. Drury's bookshop had sold many copies. I was surprised to find Scipio disagreeing and I did not understand why. I had read the book and considered it on balance a practical not a religious book, advocating freedom and the right to participate in government. A book, in fact, that championed a fairer system in which someone like me would have a better chance. I made a mental note to read it again more carefully. Meanwhile I made an effort to mediate. "Why don't you draft the address, Will, and I'll ask if Dr Darwin will look at it?" I said.

The day of the meeting at the Talbot Inn arrived. I persuaded Scipio to come with me as a guest. We scuttled down the street in the rain, squeezed ourselves in (I had never realised that the Society had so many members) and sat down in a corner out of the way next to the haberdasher and a cobbler.

Clearly the unseasonable weather had not put anyone off. Respectable trades people, artisans and shopkeepers made up the bulk of the members I saw around me. I suspected it was they who were responsible for the steady sales of the *Mercury*. On an improvised platform were the leading lights of the Society. It was easy to recognise the vast bulk of Dr Darwin himself, perched precariously on a chair that looked far too delicate for the task of supporting the great man, and I also knew the Strutt brothers and Mr Crompton by sight. The chairman introduced Will after some preamble although he really needed no introduction by now; he had become a prominent and popular feature of Derby political life.

Will stepped up to the lectern provided and began his well-rehearsed speech in a voice that was clear, steady and audible to the back of the room. He started the introduction to his address in words that sounded bold but by no means revolutionary:

"Fellow citizens, claiming it as our indefeasible right to associate together, in a peaceable and friendly manner, for the communication of thoughts, the formation of opinions, and to promote the general happiness ..."

I glanced at Scipio. We had heard all this before, of course, in rehearsal, but he seemed reassured. "So far so good," his expression seemed to say.

"... We think, therefore, that the cause of truth and justice can never be hurt by temperate and honest discussions, and that cause which will not bear such a scrutiny, must be systematically or practically bad. "

The tradespeople continued listening intently, their damp outer clothes steaming a little as the temperature in the room began to rise. Will moved on to his "Seven Point Declaration" which was to be a kind of manifesto for the society. What would they think? Would they agree with him or would they line up at the end to cancel their subscriptions? As for me, I was glad to be sitting listening for once to an address by someone who would not stir up my strange anxiety about how one can "know Jesus" but concentrate his remarks instead on more practical matters.

In fact, Will's proposals were deliberately calculated not to refer to religious matters or anything else that might divide his hearers. He covered his points, moving steadily from the "purpose of government being the happiness of the citizens" through the "reduction of taxation" and the "folly of war" to matters of "equal representation of all citizens" and the "annual election of parliaments". All these objectives were to be reached, of course, by peaceful means. His tone was rational and measured. I looked around. There was no sign of disagreement on the faces that surrounded me.

Even Scipio, reassured perhaps by, "we are ... fully sensible, that our situation is comfortable, compared with that of the people of many European kingdoms; and that as the times are in some degree moderate, they ought to be free from riot and confusion," seemed content.

Then Will advanced to more dangerous stuff. As the pungent scent of damp wool began to permeate the room, he compared the English situation with what was happening in France. Flushed with the feeling of personal success, he was really letting himself go. He was an natural orator and was warming to his theme.

"And when we cast our eyes across the channel to a people just formed in a free community, without having had time to grow rich, under a Government by which justice is duly administered, the poor taught and comforted, property protected, taxes few and easy, and that at a small expense – we ask ourselves – 'Are we in England? – have our forefathers fought, and bled, and conquered for liberty? – And did not they think that the fruits of their patriotism would be more abundant in peace, plenty, and happiness?'"

How would that go down? Hints at a reduction of taxes are generally popular with those who pay them. Drier now, the listeners were more comfortable and, as I looked around me, I saw widespread expressions of agreement. Now Will was drawing to his conclusion. "Lastly – we invite the friends of freedom throughout Great Britain to form similar societies, and to act with unanimity and firmness, till the people are too wise to be imposed upon; and their influence in the government is equal to their dignity and importance." He paused dramatically then came to a rousing climax, "Then, *and not until then,* shall we be free and happy!"

The audience rose to its feet, united. The weather outside was completely forgotten. Even Scipio, carried away for the moment at least, stood up. The applause (there were no shouts or whistles) was loudly enthusiastic and polite but sustained; in fact, I thought they would never stop.

The rain had stopped when at last we streamed out of the Talbot Inn. In the warmth of the summer night we made our way down the street towards Scipio's den at the print-shop, part of the dispersing company. "What do you think?" asked Scipio, as the crowd thinned out. "*Is* the purpose of government the general happiness and prosperity of all honest citizens?"

This seemed self-evident to me. The alternative was surely that its purpose was unhappiness for some or the happiness and prosperity only of those with most power – and that could not be right. "What do you think, then?" I asked in surprise. "That it is *not* so?"

"The purpose of government is to restrain evil, promote good and so carry out God's will," said Scipio, "in my opinion."

The address appeared in the *Mercury* the following day. Mr Drury's shop at Market Head sold out of copies at once. But that was only the beginning. Dr Darwin had a friend in Paris, a Dr Johnson, who had it read out to the National Assembly itself! They liked it, he said. There was talk of presenting it to Parliament in London but whether that ever happened or not I don't remember now because a much more local matter claimed all our attention.

Dr Darwin's close friend and neighbour in Full Street was Mr William Strutt, son of the mill owner and inventor of the Derby Rib Stocking Machine, Jedediah Strutt. He had been on the platform on the evening of Will's address. Not the most perceptive of men, he began to energetically distribute Tom Paine's *Rights of Man* among his mill workers. They did not like it. In fact they hated it and one November morning the Strutt family woke to find that their mill had been deliberately flooded and the copies of Paine's book burned.

"Why do they object to the book so much?" I asked Scipio. "Isn't Paine advocating freedom for them? They have no votes, no say in the government. Surely he is on their side!"

We were in the shop together. It was past closing time and Scipio was shelving new stock behind the counter. The smart new-smelling leather on the spines of clean volumes glowed in the warm light of the lamp on the counter: the gold lettering shone. Scipio paused and straightened his back. "Have you forgotten the Birmingham riots, Matt?" he asked. "The mill workers may not have a deep understanding of Bible teaching but they do object to having the Strutt family force their unorthodox religious opinions on them just because they are their employers."

"What do you mean?" I asked. "Religious opinions? What has Paine to do with religion?"

"Everything," he answered. "The Strutts are leading members of the Friargate Chapel. They have the same views as Dr Priestley whose house the Birmingham rioters burnt down. The mill workers object to having Paine's books forced on them because they make a connection between Paine's ideas, his religious beliefs and those of the Strutts. Paine is a Deist – according to him, some Supreme Being just set the world going and then left it alone. The Strutts at Friargate Chapel and Dr Priestley at Birmingham may not always go quite that far but they have left the idea of Jesus Christ being God far behind them. The mill workers are no more exact in their judgments than the rioters. All they know is that Paine is a heretic and so are the Strutts. They work for the Strutts but they do not want to be told to think like them."

Doctor Darwin's flattering words, "You, Matthew, will come to this understanding also," rose up in my mind and I was conscious of a faintly uneasy feeling. I recognised the ideas that Scipio was describing as those the Doctor had outlined to me, although he had taken them further, even suggesting the method by which the "Supreme Being" had acted.

"It seems a distant connection," I objected.

"On the contrary," replied Scipio, "it is at the heart of the matter."

December brought more sensational events. Will's Address became even more notorious. *The London Morning Chronicle* got hold of a copy and published it on Christmas morning. Mercifully for Will, as it turned out, his name appeared nowhere in the paper. By this time things in France were changing in a way that worried even Will. No longer were moderate men like Will's hero, Pastor Jean-Paul Rabaut, in control. The French dethroned their king and put him on trial as plain Citizen Louis Capet. France was declared a Republic with an elected National Convention. Votes for all men had been introduced but fear of violence prevented many from voting at all. France was now in the grip of brutality.

The British government was alarmed, as were most British people. Politics were turning ugly across the channel. Ordinary people from mill workers to shop keepers shuddered with horror at the thought of such things happening to their own beloved King George III, whose kindness was a byword. Those who had expressed ideas capable of even mildly republican interpretation were now strongly suspected of disloyalty. Indeed *any* criticism of the government was liable to be taken for republicanism in this uncomfortable climate.

January brought more unwelcome developments. One freezing morning with snow in the air I set off for the dispensary knowing it would be crowded. There would be people wanting advice about children with coughs and old grandmothers who in reality were just not able to keep warm. I was out early so on my way I called in on the *Mercury* Office. I knew the mails would be in and I was always keen to hear the latest news from London and from France.

"I'm beginning to wish I'd listened to your advice, Scipio," said Will as we stood together in Scipio's little basement cubbyhole before the shop opened. "I should have spoken more moderately. There was no need to sound like a republican. I never intended a word against good King George. I wish the French would get a grip on themselves. They won't seem to listen to Pastor Rabaut any more – it is as if they are going mad! If they are not careful they'll ruin everything they've done and stop us getting reform here too. Let's hope there is better news in the this post that can go in the *Mercury* tomorrow. Here Scipio, can you scan through these? The boy from the Bell just brought them in from last night's London mail." And he passed Scipio some of the papers and began to open another packet himself.

I wrapped my muffler more tightly round my neck ready to go on my way and leave the newspaper staff to get on with their job when Will gave a cry of horror. He sat down on a chair with a bump. "Oh no, Matt, Scipio, look! The government are prosecuting the owners of *The Morning Chronicle* in London for seditious libel for publishing my *Address!* If they are found guilty they'll be transported!" The room suddenly felt even colder.

"Hmm," said Scipio quietly, looking up from some pages that he had spread on the desk where he did his accounts, "and the French have put their king to death. He was guillotined on Monday."

Chapter six

THE MORNING CHRONICLE

1793

With fostering peace the suffering nations bless,
And guard the freedom of the immortal Press!

(Erasmus Darwin, The Temple of Nature)

*P*ost after post brought worse news from France and with each post the prospect of *The Morning Chronicle* proprietors being acquitted seemed to recede further and further. Post after post also brought news of the reaction of our government in London to events in France. And events in France – violence, bloodshed, the guillotine, all religion outlawed in favour of a new religion with festivals of worship directed to the Supreme Being – added weight to Scipio's views.

The government in London was taking steps to ensure nothing of the kind even began to develop in Britain. They threatened to take away the licences of inn-keepers who allowed their premises to be used for meetings such as the one that had taken place at the Talbot. It was said they were seizing mail destined for men they considered possible sources of trouble. Then there was the Aliens Act. This was aimed at preventing French revolutionary agitators coming into Britain by identifying them at the ports of entry.

Will had been horrified that someone else was in trouble for what he had written. "I've reported the prosecution in the *Mercury* just verbatim from the London papers without saying who wrote the Address but I had better own up," he said, as we sat in Scipio's cosy cubbyhole discussing the question. "I wrote it: if anyone gets transported, it should be me."

"Before you do anything rash," said Scipio, "make sure it will make a difference to the outcome. You may find that all it means, is that you will go to Botany Bay in a convict ship along with Mr Perry, Mr Lambert and Mr Gray of *The Morning Chronicle* if there is a conviction."

After my work at the dispensary that morning I was tucking into a steak and kidney pudding in the kitchen – one of Mrs B's best – a melting suet pastry, soft and toothsome, full of tender beef and rich, aromatic gravy. Dr Darwin himself ate very little meat. Mrs B was adept at creating cheese dishes and tempting vegetable creations as well as sweet pastries and fruit pies for him. How anyone could turn down a pudding like this in favour of a salad, even a salad prepared by Mrs B, was beyond my comprehension. But then, there had been so little meat in my childhood that perhaps I exaggerated its importance. Mrs B herself was not in the kitchen and I pulled my copy of the *Rights of Man* out of my pocket to peruse as I ate.

I had assumed Dr Darwin was still out on his morning rounds so I was lingering over the last few mouthfuls as I read, thinking I had plenty of time to prepare his study for a particular experiment he was conducting. Suddenly the familiar voice stammered out of the speaking tube by the fireplace: "S-send M-Matthew up, p-please, C-Cook."

I jumped up, almost upsetting my now empty plate, brushed the pudding crumbs hastily from my lap and stuffed the *Rights of Man* back into my pocket.

"I'm sorry, Sir," I said as I entered the study, "I assumed you were not yet home or I would have ..."

He waved me to a chair. "You m-must know about this already," he said pointing to a copy of the *Mercury* on his desk. I knew at once which article he referred to.

"Yes, Sir," I said. "And I am glad to have the opportunity to discuss it with you."

He raised his eyebrows.

"Will – that is Mr Ward – is very distressed and talks of owning up to having written it. Would that be a good course of action, Sir?"

"C-certainly n-not!" said the Doctor briskly. "No n-need to add another victim to the s-sacrifice – even assuming there was a m-mechanism by which he c-could do s-such a thing! N-no. I have a c-course of action in m-mind. G-go over and ask Mr W-Ward to step up here if he w-would be s-so k-kind, M-Matthew, and I c-can explain it t-to him."

"I have been d-discussing the m-matter with Mr S-Strutt," said Dr Darwin, when Will arrived, "and I s-suggested that Mr Erskine be engaged to d-defend the pr-proprietors of the *Chronicle*. We are agreed that he is well qu-qualified for the t-task. Mr S-Strutt is engaged in writing to Mr P-Perry of the *Chronicle* – and to M-Mr Erskine – n-now."

"Mr Erskine!" Will exclaimed in a voice of awe, "The famous lawyer who defended Paine's *Rights of Man!* The man that was cheered to the skies after the case? The crowds unhitched the horses from his carriage afterwards, didn't they? They pulled it themselves shouting, 'Down with Paine but Erskine for ever,' and 'The Liberty of the Press; the King, the Constitution, *and Erskine* for ever' – or something like that ... surely he wouldn't ... I mean he ... "

"Yes, b-but he *lost* the c-case, remember," said the Doctor dryly, "and it is b-by no m-means g-guaranteed that he will w-win this one. However, if anyone c-can s-succeed he w-will."

"But the costs, Sir!" exclaimed Will. "The proprietors of the *Chronicle* ..."

"Shall n-not have to b-bear them," interrupted the Doctor. "Mr S-Strutt will p-put up the m-money."

"I said that young m-man will g-go far," said the Doctor when the discussions were over and Will had left, still faltering out his thanks, "and I d-did n-not mean to B-Botany B-Bay!"

The case against *The Morning Chronicle* did not come on until December. By that time things in France were worse than ever. Parisians were pulled away from their families and homes on the word of some informer and sent to the guillotine with a mere mockery of a trial. The hideous theatrical of death seemed to play on and on without so much as an intermission in the performance. To crown it all, if that is not an unfortunate expression, the French declared war on England. Sympathy with revolutionary France now looked exactly like treason.

On the Sunday morning before *The Morning Chronicle* trial, all three of us were at the chapel. I was a little late that morning and I squeezed past Mrs Brown from the farm who was sitting beside Susan, both in their Sunday-best bonnets. I slid gratefully into the space between Scipio and Will that they had kept for me. The chapel was finished now. Pale winter sunlight poured through tall glazed windows and there was even a stove to keep the chill of early December out of the building.

That morning Mr Archer preached a rousing sermon on some words of the Apostle Paul about counting everything except knowing Christ as a loss.

Mr Archer's preaching was variable. Sometimes I did not understand a word of it, but today he was crystal clear and the topic was the one that had puzzled me since I first started to go to the services at Agard Street. Again and again I had puzzled over those words, *"knowing Christ"*, *"knowing* the Saviour". They always stuck in my mind and I never understood them. We could know *about* Christ, yes, but how could we know Him?

"Now Paul does not mean by 'the knowledge of Christ,' just knowing the things that Christ taught," said Mr Archer. "We can look down to verse ten and see that he means we can know Him personally."

That was exactly the part I did not understand! I nudged Will to indicate that I thought something important was coming up but he had an anxious, far away look on his face; clearly something else was on his mind. I was not surprised. The trial he was so much dreading was set to begin in London the very next day.

"We may know Him," continued Mr Archer earnestly. "And this knowledge of Christ, is closely connected with our knowledge of the three persons of the One Deity. The Bible tells us that there are three who bear record in heaven, by whose grace, love and fellowship we are blessed. It is only through revelation, through the Bible, that we can know this. But just because we cannot know it without having it revealed to us by God's written word does not mean it is not true. Surely God is not restricted to writing in His Word only things that we could have understood without it!"

Will was twisting his hat round and round listlessly in his hands. He seemed to droop, looking down at the floor. I looked away from this uninspiring and uncharacteristic behaviour and listened on, eagerly hoping to understand what came next, whether Will was taking it in or not.

"Nor does this concept deserve to be rejected just because it is mysterious. Natural philosophers find mysteries in the nature of every creature, and it would be strange if there were none in the nature of our Creator Himself!"

I was well acquainted with one natural philosopher, Dr Darwin, of course. His study of anatomy, animals, and plants included every aspect of nature. Yet I knew that there were indeed things in nature which he did not understand and that other scientists did not understand either. A sentence that I had copied for the Doctor from his notes just the other day popped into my mind: "The mystery of reproduction, which alone distinguishes organic life from mechanic or chemic action, *is yet wrapped in darkness.*" No one understood this mystery and many others like it; Mr Archer was correct, although he knew nothing about medicine – or any other branch of science.

He was warming to his theme now and despite the comfortable smell of hot metal from the new stove I was not in the least drowsy. "Indeed His very existence, eternity, and infinity, surpass our comprehension just as truly as the Trinity does. Shall we who do not understand the union of soul and body; the motion of our own limbs, or the growth of a blade of grass, refuse to believe the account God has given us of Himself? No, we believe, according to Scripture, that Jesus is God's own, proper Son; the only-begotten of the Father ..."

The Trinity! This was the other thing that had been puzzling me but I did not nudge Will's limp arm again. Was Mr Archer saying that *no one* really understood it? No surprise that I found it impossible then; that I could not take in this idea of Jesus being God *and* God's own Son at the same time.

Scipio's explanation of the reaction of the workers in Strutts' mill came back to my mind. This was the thing that the Strutts and their friends at Friargate Chapel did *not* believe and as for Paine and his *Rights of Man* – only pure unaided human reason was of any use to Paine. I could imagine him scoffing at the very idea that it was unimportant that human beings could not understand the nature of God.

"... To whom He says, 'Thy throne O GOD is for ever and ever ... for by Him were all things created' as the apostle writes. By Him, and for Him, notice that! 'He is before all things, and by Him all things consist.' How absurd it would be to suppose it could be said of a mere created being that all things were made by him, and for him! No Christ is not a created being – He is God!"

Scipio was a picture of happy concentration nodding his agreement but on the other side of me Will now seemed to be staring out of the nearest of the chapel's lofty new windows, his mind completely elsewhere. Mr Archer was at his most logical and Will was missing it all! Then I caught sight of his full face for a moment and I was astonished. Will was grey and haggard with grief like a mourner at a funeral.

"Come and welcome to Jesus Christ." Mr Archer was saying. "He that hath no money, may come, and receive a full supply for all his necessities, without money and without price. We are commanded to invite all that we meet. Come! Him that cometh unto Me I will in no wise cast out, says Jesus." And now I seemed to have lost him again. What was this all about? What was the connection? I must have missed something. Determined, I did not let my mind drift off as I usually did when I couldn't follow. I kept listening, hoping that somewhere further on I would grasp what it was about. I was not disappointed. The next point was practical and easy to comprehend – up to a point.

"But, do you ask, 'Am I a believer?' Examine yourselves, whether ye be in the faith. Christ must be in you, and you in Him."

I was going to go back to Full Street for my dinner and I confess that usually, by the time we reached the closing hymn at Agard Street, it was what Mrs B would have waiting for me on the kitchen table that was uppermost in my mind. Today, however, it was different. Mr Archer had given me something to chew on. Was I a believer? Did it matter? How should I "examine myself"? Above all, what did it mean this "come to Jesus"?

As we stood up to sing, something else flashed through my mind. How did Christ as creator fit with the Doctor's grand theory of a Great First Cause? Whatever Mr Archer said, I was anxious not to jeopardize the scientific knowledge that had put me on the first step of the ladder to my ambition.

Dr Darwin had trusted me with his ideas. I dared to hope that membership of the Lunar Society would one day be within my grasp. It would be best to keep these scientific matters separate from chapel affairs, I decided. After all, scientific, philosophical enquiry was not a religious matter. There could surely be no tension between these two unrelated things. As far as religious matters went, I was more perplexed than ever but I was confident that I was beginning to grasp the inner workings of science. It takes a long time to write this down but I had followed the whole train of thought before we had even opened our mouths for the first verse.

We sang, "Come, let us join our cheerful songs with angels round the throne", and I stole another glance at poor Will. He was making no effort to sing the words which so obviously jarred with his frame of mind.

Scipio disappeared after the service before I reached the back of the chapel or I would have put to him the questions that were troubling me. He often went back to the farm on a Sunday for dinner with Farmer and Mrs Brown. I would have to rely on my other friend. From his behaviour in chapel I wondered if Will had heard, never mind understood, Mr Archer. Still, there was no harm in trying. "Will," I began as we walked along Agard Street together, "Can you explain what Mr Archer meant?" but he seemed not to hear. "Will, what's the matter? Are you feeling poorly?"

He shook himself. "No ... no, Matt. Sorry, I did not sleep well last night."

"Not sleep well? What was the matter? Is it the trial?" Will had a reputation for sleeping like a log which Scipio and I put down to the amount of energy he expended during his waking hours. If he was losing sleep, *The Morning Chronicle* affair was obviously hitting him harder than I had expected.

"No ... that is ... I'm afraid there is rather bad news from Paris."

I wondered how there could be any news from Paris worse than that which we had heard in a steady stream over the last months. "Bad news?"

"Yes. Poor Pastor Rabaut ... on Thursday ... he was sent to the guillotine. He's dead, Matt."

Chapter Seven

THE EVE OF THE
REFORM MEETING

1793-4

Ye patriot heroes! in the glorious cause,
Of Justice, Mercy, Liberty, and Laws,
Who call to Virtue's shrine the British youth,
And shake the senate with the voice of Truth;
Rouse the dull ear, the hoodwink'd eye unbind,
And give to energy the public mind ...

(Erasmus Darwin, The Temple Of Nature)

*W*ill's news had been gleaned from correspondence which had reached him on Saturday night. The trial was to start on Monday and the death of Monsieur Rabaut now hung over us like a horrible omen. By Wednesday Will was haunting the Bell Inn watching for the mails like someone waiting for the blade of the guillotine to fall.

"M-much hangs on the result," Dr Darwin agreed. I had been carrying on with my work on the draft of *Zoonomia* that morning while he was out on his rounds and the numbered sheets lay on the desk covered with my careful script.

"Would Will himself be in danger, if Mr Perry and his colleagues are convicted, Sir?" I asked.

"If the p-paper's p-proprietors were c-convicted and t-transported, yes," the Doctor replied frankly. "I'm afraid everyone in the D-Derby S-Society for P-Political Information knows who read the address at the m-meeting; it c-can't be k-kept s-secret. The *D-Derby M-Mercury* p-published it first, too and W-William W-Ward is the editor. Now that B-Britain and F-France are at w-war also, the Address ap-ppears in a m-more s-serious l-light."

"Would Mr Drury be prosecuted too if Mr Perry and his friends were convicted then?"

"We c-cannot rule that out. In S-Scotland two g-good m-men have already b-been t-transported for p-publishing the s-same ideas."

I shivered. Kind Mr Drury sent to Botany Bay; Will himself transported. Such things could not happen, surely, could they?

When my work was finished that day I set out to hurry round the corner and across the market place to the printers to find out if there was any news. The wind whipped across the empty market and in the halos of light round the street oil-lamps, slanting lines of sleety rain glistened. Head down and hurrying into the cold blast I almost bumped into Scipio as I turned into Irongate.

"I have excellent news for you!" He was elated and his usually firm voice had an uncharacteristic tremor. "Acquitted! Not guilty! I was coming to tell you. Will has just received a court abstract in the mail; it came in just a few minutes ago ... "

Together we clattered into the warmth of the print shop. Will had papers spread out over the counter. They were covered in a spidery hand that showed evidence of haste. With a shaking finger he pointed to the foot of the last page:

"... the special verdict was, Guilty Of Publishing, But Not With Malicious Intent. Lord Kenyon: 'I cannot record this verdict; it is no verdict at all.' The jury then withdrew and, after sitting in discussion till about five in the morning, they found a general verdict of – Not Guilty."

"Not Guilty ..." I whispered the words.

Scipio's excitement had subsided now. It was he who suggested we should give God thanks and it was he that spoke the grateful words when we three bowed our heads.

"Dr Darwin, Mr Strutt!" I exclaimed. "They need to know!"

"Yes," said Will at once, "Here, Matt," and he folded the sheets up, "take these across to the Doctor with my grateful thanks. He and Mr Strutt should have them not I. I've read enough to put something together for the *Mercury*."

When Dr Darwin had digested the contents of the hastily written sheets, he directed me to make a copy and then went straight out to call on his neighbour Mr Strutt.

I stored up the details in my mind as I wrote, thinking that I could share them with Scipio and Will who had had less time to study the paper than I. Will's name was not mentioned and it seems that even Mr Erskine, the lawyer, had had no knowledge of who had written the address. As I copied away industriously it emerged that at the trial Mr Erskine had hinted that the address was by Dr Darwin himself. "This paper is rumoured to come from the pen of a writer, whose productions justly entitle him to rank as the first poet of the age ..." I found myself carefully copying: it was a reference to Dr Darwin's popular, though anonymous, book of poetry, *The Botanic Garden*.

I called at the newspaper shop after closing the dispensary. Will was still closeted in his own office working away at a graphic article about the horrors of the so-called "middle passage," the actual slave-carrying part, of the slave traders' triangular voyage. When I told Scipio that Mr Erskine thought the address had been written by Dr Darwin he smiled.

"He did give Will some hints," he said, "but I can't imagine them squeezing Dr Darwin into a convict ship, if they went on to prosecute him as the author, that is."

I agreed. "There is so much of Dr Darwin they'd have to leave half the other convicts behind to make room," I said with a smile.

"What do you think of the Doctor's ideas, Matt?" asked Scipio. "I mean, I know you are grateful to him for what you learn about medicine but I understand there are other things ..."

"Oh, I'm very grateful indeed," I said, "and he is a first rate doctor despite being interested, as you say, in so many other areas of science. He does his own research too – on all sorts of topics."

"Oh, I did not mean that his interest in science has a bad effect on his abilities as a physician," began Scipio, "I was merely commenting on his philosophical ideas ..."

I sensed where this was leading. "Look," I said, "I have no money. The doctor knows that I cannot go to study in Edinburgh to be a physician. It does not mean that I could not set up as an apothecary like Mr Cook or Mr Harrison, though. I have free run of the Doctor's medical books and he teaches me himself freely in return for my services. I get all the latest medical knowledge even though I don't have any hope of qualifying. Many of the Doctor's famous friends had a poor start in life and had to learn the hard way. I see no reason why I should not use my brains and get on and I'm determined to do so." I drew a deep breath. "You know we live in times of change, Scipio. The doctor's ideas are the way forward. They are ideas in the field of science, natural philosophy, not religion."

"But Matt," persisted Scipio, who had obviously been reading some of Dr Darwin's poetry books in the shop when business was slack, "what do you think of the *ideas,* whatever field they cover – the ideas in his poems for instance?"

"He quotes the Bible in his books," I said, realising that it was religious ideas that Scipio was determined to discuss. "He is no atheist; he certainly believes in God. He says that God is the Great Architect of the Universe. He has discovered, he says, that the earth in the beginning was covered with water, since some of its highest mountains consist of shells cemented together. That means that animal life began beneath the sea."

"I can think of a simpler explanation for water all over the earth," murmured Scipio, "and it relates to Noah ..." but I ignored his remark and continued, "This animal life was originally what he calls a living point, fibre or filament that had the power to change. The development was slow and gradual over maybe millions of years."

"And how does he think he knows this?" asked Scipio.

"Well, he says we see changes in life all around us. Caterpillars change into butterflies. Over generations animals can be bred with different features and abilities from their parents. After islands or continents were raised above the first ocean, great numbers of the most simple animals would look for food at the edges of this new land. So they might gradually become amphibious. He gives the example of the frog which does this even today and the gnat which changes from a swimming to a flying creature. There is a great similarity of structure, in all the warm-blooded animals, birds, amphibious animals and mankind. He comes to the conclusion therefore that they have all been produced from an original living filament through small changes over millions of ages of time."

"But do you think this is correct?" Scipio persisted and there was a strange tone in his voice.

"I think it is likely," I replied. "You know yourself how tiny creatures – maggots and so on – just appear when things rot. That would explain how things started. Then one can imagine a great procession of creatures," I continued expansively, " first crawling out of the ocean then becoming amphibious like the frog, then walking like the reptiles and mammals which developed further bringing ..."

"... bringing the apes and monkeys," continued Scipio in a very soft, even tone, "which developed into Africans like me and then, finally, the pinnacle of creation, people like you ..."

There was an embarrassed silence. This stark observation put a finger on something I had not yet thought out.

"Well," I mumbled, "that's not necessarily ... that is, I don't think ..."

"The Bible says God made everything in *six days,*" Scipio said quietly. "Not millions of years."

I did not enjoy being baldly confronted with this, especially by Scipio. It jarred. It was incongruous, irritating almost, and I wanted to avoid it. Scipio, an ex-slave, was my good friend yet I liked Dr Darwin's impressive ideas and I liked the way he thought things out for himself. Beside him Mr Archer, for instance, was unimaginative, dull and predictable. If I was going to get on in the world it seemed to me that Dr Darwin's theories were likely to prevail over more old-fashioned ideas.

"We do not insult God if we say that He made the creation we see around us by a long and gradual process," I pointed out, defending myself with the lesson I had learned from the Doctor. "For if so, He must then have created the process of creation itself which is a greater marvel than just creating things as they are."

"I'm not considering, for the moment, whether or not we *insult* Him," said Scipio. "I'm speaking about whether or not we even *believe* Him – believe what He says in the Bible. What you have been telling me is the opposite of what we read there – in Genesis. I say 'Let God be true and every man a liar'."

That night Scipio's words returned to trouble me. Surely it must be possible, I reasoned to myself as I lay on my bed in the little attic at Full Street, to accept the reasoned deductions of science without turning your back on the Bible. Yet what Scipio said was disturbing. Did I have to abandon the Bible or at least question it if I wanted to follow the Doctor's views? I turned over and, with a sigh, consigned the whole issue to the big bag of problems that Matthew Batchelor could not solve, along with the Trinity and the idea of knowing Jesus personally. Perhaps, I thought, these were things too hard for human reason at all and best left alone – especially by someone who was determined to better himself.

Will's spirits had lifted after the outcome of the trial. He was no longer weighed down with the thought of the prosecution and its ramifications should Mr Perry and his friends be convicted. Despite worse and worse news pouring in from France, he was soon laying more plans to further the cause of parliamentary reform. One bitter cold evening just after Christmas I was clearing up in the dispensary. The last shivering enquirer had departed when Will blew in with the freezing wind, full of excitement.

"Mr Thelwall is coming to Derby!" he said, gleefully waving a letter. "I asked him to address a meeting and he says he will come."

As I had never heard of this gentleman, I could not, at first, share the excitement. "Mr who?" I asked.

"Thelwall! He is a poet and an expert on ... on ... 'animal vitality', I think it is called – whatever it is that makes living things ... er ... well ... live."

"Animality?" I supplied helpfully for I knew the term from the Doctor's writings.

"Yes, that's probably it. Dr Darwin will know of him. I think their ideas are similar. Thelwall is an expert on correct speaking and shorthand writing and oh, all sorts of interesting things."

This sounded not quite Will's usual area of enthusiasm nor did I see why it would form the subject of an address to a public meeting.

"What is he going to talk to a meeting about, then?" I asked, rather hoping it would perhaps be the abolition of slavery that Will was so keen on and not another dangerous address like the one that had just caused so much trouble. But Will had not learned his lesson.

"Oh, he is a great advocate of parliamentary reform, that's the subject of his addresses – votes for everyone, annual parliaments and that sort of thing," he explained. "I think he would go down so well here. Just what we need to get things going again. There has been a definite flagging of interest here in Derby since *The Morning Chronicle* affair. Mr Thelwall is a very accomplished orator. He goes round addressing meetings everywhere. But come over to the newspaper shop, if you've finished here, and I'll show you his speeches; I have some in my office."

Not for the first time, Will's enthusiasm for dangerous enterprises amazed me. He seemed quite to have forgotten that not long before the "flagging of interest" he had been close to qualifying for a long one-way sea voyage at government expense! I raked the cold ash out of the dispensary grate, left a note from Dr Darwin to Dr Pigot where I knew he would see it in the morning and followed Will to the newspaper office. Here in the winter evenings Will, Scipio and I were in the habit of enjoying a bag of chestnuts roasted on a shovel over the stove. I was surprised to find that Scipio was absent tonight.

"Oh, he's up at the Browns' farm again this evening," said Will, in reply to my question, "always off there these days he is. Here now, this is a report of Thelwall's latest address." And he unfolded a London newspaper for me to read while he poked the stove into action and pricked the chestnuts ready to spread them out on the shovel.

The delicious warm fragrance of charring chestnut shells began to reach my nostrils as I scanned the page. "He's certainly a fiery orator!" I conceded when I had read my fill. "'Enormous mill-stone of debts – contracted without the consent of the honest labourers who have no vote – industrious poor – unrepresented and paying for the disgrace, defeat, reproach, infamy and misery of war ...' He makes a strong case."

"Yes, and the audiences lap it up," replied Will, peeling a scalding chestnut cautiously. "He is very careful in everything he says in public; he won't get *his* fingers burnt if he can help it – ouch!" He blew on his own scorched fingertips and added, "but he is clear on the need for reform: votes for everyone, fair distribution of parliamentary seats and so on."

This was reassuring. "Where will you hold the meeting?" I asked, as I tackled my own chestnut gingerly. "The landlord of the Talbot won't welcome you again. You know he might lose his licence as a consequence now."

"Oh, I'll use the chapel," said Will airily.

On the evening of the meeting the three of us were in Mr Drury's roomy office. Mr Thelwall had arrived the previous day and was staying at the Bell.

"Mr Archer did not mind you using the chapel, then?" asked Scipio.

"No. Well, that is," admitted Will, "I have not actually asked him. He was not in when I called yesterday but it will be fine I'm sure. I've got the keys from the chapel keeper."

Scipio raised his eyebrows. "But Will, suppose ..."

"It will be fine!" reiterated Will, "Mr Drury's a chapel member: he knows what is going on. Why would Mr Archer object? Is Dr Darwin coming to the meeting, Matt? We can put a seat for him on the platform if so."

I was not sure about the Doctor. He had wanted to be at the meeting but he had been called out and was not back when I left Full Street. Like Scipio, I also wondered about Mr Archer. I had taken the trouble to look up some of Mr Thelwall's speeches in the little library of books and pamphlets held by the Derby Society for Political Information. I could not for a moment imagine that Mr Archer would endorse the scathing pronouncements about religion they contained. But before I could say anything Mr Drury put his head round the door.

"Will," he said, "Can I have Mr Thelwall's notes for his speech? I need to take them with me to the meeting and it is time I was off."

Will went to the big old desk and opened the secret drawer. "We put Mr Thelwall's notes for the speech in here," he explained to us as he rummaged deep in the drawer for the papers. "Just to make sure they were safe. Now where is that last page ... Oh!"

Will had pushed his hand into the very back of the secret drawer and as he did so there was a loud click, something shot forward from the back of the desk itself and before our astonished eyes the whole open flat surface of the desk was covered in a mass of jewels, gold rings, coins and pearls, winking and glistening in the light of the oil lamp.

No one moved except Scipio who crossed briskly over to the window opposite, put up the shutters and barred them.

Chapter eight

RIOT

1794

Demoniac Envy scowls with haggard mien,
And blights the bloom of other's joys, unseen;
Or wrathful Jealousy invades the grove,
And turns to night meridian beams of Love!

(Erasmus Darwin, The Temple of Nature)

*T*here was a moment of astounded silence. A new-minted gold half guinea rolled across the front of the desk, knocking into a little gold trinket shaped like a crescent moon. They fell onto the stone floor together. Then Mr Drury said, "Congratulations, Matthew, you are a rich man, after all."

Will picked up the shining new coin. *"Georgius Secundus Dei Gratia,"* he read and turned the coin over. "Seventeen-forty-five." And then he thumped me on the back very hard and there were tears in his eyes.

I was totally uncomprehending. "But it is not mine ..." I stammered. I bent and picked up the trinket.

"It is indeed yours," said Mr Drury at once. "That desk was bought from your grandmother by my Uncle Samuel when he owned the *Mercury*. He bought the desk, not your grandmother's er ... other belongings that she and he had no idea were in it."

For a moment I saw my grandmother in my mind's eye: the cold cheerless room, the dear old face lined with worry, the cheeks pinched. She had been dependent on the kindness of others even for the few sticks that burned in her grate ... And all the time, all that money was all hers and she had no idea at all where it was.

Scipio was examining the drawer. "I see how it is done," he said. "Look, you push the back of the drawer and it releases this hidden spring that pushes the whole of the false back of the desk forwards. No wonder it was such a heavy piece of furniture with all that gold inside it!"

I sat down on a chair, shocked, dazed. "But is it ... is it mine?"

"It is yours," said Mr Drury again firmly, "and I suggest that, since the meeting is about to start at any minute and I have the speaker's notes here in my hand, we simply put it all back where it came from, for the moment. Then when the meeting is over we can help you count it, if you wish, and you can get some advice as to how to invest it or bank it, sell the jewels or whatever. Dr Darwin will help you, I'm sure, and so will Mr Archer if you ask him – he is a banker."

"It has been safe there for nearly fifty years," said Will, "so it will be safe for a couple of hours more. How does this thing work, Scipio?" And he began to shovel the jangling hoard of coins and jewels back into the space from which they had appeared. Still in a state of shock, I put the little gold moon into my pocket. Along its raised centre, a line of tiny diamonds sparked in the light of the lamp. The lunar shape was a talisman. I was going to be eligible for the Doctor's learned society after all.

As I took my seat in the chapel, my mind was beginning to whirl. How grateful I was to Mr Drury that he was fair and generous enough to unquestioningly acknowledge me as the rightful owner! I began to see myself setting out for Edinburgh and a new life as a medical student. I knew how to be frugal. That money would see me through and, with care, start me in a medical practice. I was going to be a doctor! A university trained doctor! The Lunar Society had become a real possibility and with a smile I fingered the little crescent trinket in my pocket.

The chapel was packed. Scipio squeezed in and sat next to me with Susan from the farm on the other side of him. My thoughts were miles away. Mr Thelwall started his speech but my head was so full of plans for my new future that I did not hear a word he said. For all I heard of his address he could have been lecturing on the latest French fashion in ladies' bonnets, although I was dimly aware that Paris did get mentioned on several occasions.

The chapel was crammed to capacity and there was a noise from outside like a crowd of people all wanting to get in. At the meeting at the Talbot all those present were very well behaved subscribers to the Derby Society for Political Information. This evening's audience was different. All sorts of people appeared to be in the chapel and it was clear that neither Will nor anyone else had any idea where they had come from. Things grew lively and the unruly element began to shout comments to the speaker and heckle.

"Why don't you get some guillotines over here and have done with it?" shouted someone.

"Down with the French!" came another.

"Church and King!" came an ominous cry from somewhere else.

Mr Thelwall did not seem to mind, however, and answered every remark adroitly, hardly pausing in the flow of his speech. I had just moved on from considering what kind of comfortable lodgings I might find in Edinburgh and whether I should choose to have my meals provided or to eat in a tavern, when Scipio glanced out of the window and then rose from beside me.

"I don't like the look of this," he whispered. "Those fellows outside are picking up stones. I think someone should go out and see what's going on – perhaps call the constable. Look, Matt, if it gets ugly in here, get Susan out quickly and take her somewhere safe – say the kitchen at Full Street – and I'll come over and get her home when it has all died down." And with that he was gone.

Moments later there were shouts of "Church and King for ever!" from outside and towards the front of the chapel a crashing smashing sound as the panes of the beautiful new windows were assaulted with stones. I awoke from my reverie abruptly. For the first time I became aware that some of those inside the meeting were carrying stout sticks and even clubs. Susan! What had Scipio said? Fights were beginning to break out now inside the chapel. Impossible to get to the door. Then I noticed the chapel-keeper, white faced and terrified, sitting near the platform. There was only one thing to do.

"Quickly, Susan," I said. "Never mind that basket! Just leave it. Follow me."

I led her swiftly along the bench to the little door in the side wall that opens directly to the chapel-keeper's house. It was not locked and I almost pushed her in, followed her, slammed the door shut and began to bolt it from inside.

"Oh, Mr Matthew," she wailed. "What shall we do? My basket of food for old Mrs Chambers in Back Lane! Mistress said to be sure to take it. Where is Mr Africanus gone? Oh dear, oh dear!"

"Don't worry," I said. "Scipio – Mr Africanus – asked me to take you to Full Street if there were any difficulties at the chapel. Now, follow me."

The noise from the chapel rose in a tumultuous hubbub punctuated by the sound of more breaking glass. I knew the layout of the chapel house and I led the terrified Susan quickly through the kitchen, where the chapel-keeper's kettle innocently simmered beside the hob, through the dingy scullery with its bowls and dishcloths and out into a sort of vegetable patch. Susan clutched her skirts and tip-toed through the forlorn stalks of harvested cabbages which stood out in the moonlight, a line of ghostly sentinels. We emerged at last by the back gate. I led her through the weird night, the sound of unrestrained rioting from the chapel seeming as unreal as the plans for my future life which still kept revolving in my head. I made a wide circuit, keeping well away from the chapel, and so got her safely into Mrs B's care in the kitchen at Full Street.

"There seems to be a bit of a riot at the chapel," I told Mrs B at which she was at once all agog.

"A riot! Oh my poor dear!" and she received the tearful Susan into her ample bosom.

"My mistress's basket," wailed Susan. "The eggs are sure to be upset!"

"Who do they think they are, these rioters?" demanded Mrs B fiercely. "I'm surprised that a big fellow like that Mr Scipio – and you Matt – couldn't put paid to 'em."

"They were shouting 'Church and King forever!' like the Birmingham rioters who burned down Dr Darwin's friend's house," I began but this was obviously the wrong thing to say for Susan let out another wail. Mrs B picked up the poker.

"They won't come here, my dear," she said soothingly but still grasping the poker, "I'll see to that." Then turning to me she added, "You had better go and see what's happening, Matt. We will be safe enough here. Dr Darwin is in now and young Mr Erasmus with him too this evening."

I departed, promising to rescue the basket if I could, and set off back to the scene of the riot.

When I arrived back at the chapel, I was surprised to find it quiet. Everything was over and the rioters had melted away. Standing in a forlorn group in the lamplight outside the chapel and looking up at its broken windows were Mr Archer, Mr Drury and a very subdued Will. Mr Thelwall had evidently taken his departure. I stepped back, unwilling to become part of what would obviously be a painful conversation and they moved off round the side of the chapel, presumably to examine the extent of the damage to the other windows. I remembered Susan's basket and slipped inside to rummage under the bench where we had been sitting. There it was! Not a bit the worse for wear and still covered with a neat white cloth. I emerged from the chapel to find Mr Drury and Will. Mr Archer had gone.

"Matt!" said Will. He looked subdued and crestfallen. "At least you are unharmed!"

"No bones broken," I said cheerfully, for even a riot could not dash my spirits for long, now that my fortunes had taken such an unexpected turn for the better. "Where is Scipio?"

"Wasn't he with you?" asked Will. "Oh well, I expect he's escorting Susan back to the farm."

"No," I said, "Susan's at Full Street with Mrs B in the kitchen. She's quite safe but a bit shaken up. Scipio asked me to take her there if there was trouble and I got her out through the chapel-keeper's house. Scipio's probably back at the print shop. If we go over there now, he can go off to Full Street with this bothersome basket of Susan's." I was eager to get on with the task of counting up my new-found wealth.

"It could be worse, Matt," said Will in answer to my questions about the damage to the chapel as we walked to the print shop. "They've broken windows but at least they did not fire the place like the Birmingham mob."

I thought of my money. Perhaps I could make a small contribution to the repair – after I had counted up everything and worked out the estimated cost of going to Edinburgh and so on, of course. The idea of being able to help gave me a proud glow of satisfaction.

Scipio was not at the print shop but we were all eager to examine the treasure. Kind Mr Drury got out a brand new account book for me to list everything down in. He opened the front of the desk and Will reached into the back of the secret drawer and pushed the panel. There was a solid sounding click, the back panel of the desk shot forward – empty.

We stared at the empty desk stupidly. Will pushed the back panel again as if somehow his action would bring the right result this time but, of course, nothing appeared. Mr Drury scratched his head then felt about at the back of the desk panel but there was nothing there.

"What's gone wrong? What's happened?" I had a strange feeling of unreality and I could not believe what I saw.

"Someone's taken it," said Mr Drury hoarsely. Then he brightened. "No, no, Scipio must have moved it for some reason; where is he?"

I hurried back to Full Street to see if Scipio had appeared there. Of course, I would not mention the treasure in front of Mrs B and Susan. I would just say, "Scipio, did you move anything ...?"

He was not there.

For the first time that evening Susan had hysterics. "Where is Mr Africanus, then?" she cried in distress. "We ... we ... that is we had an ... an ... understanding. Oh dear, oh dear, what has happened to him?"

Edward, the gardener's lad, a strapping fellow, strong as an ox and about as clever, was summoned to take her home and Mrs B promised to deliver the basket to Mrs Chambers of Back Lane personally.

"I'll take it tomorrow, dear," she soothed. "That great black fellow can take care of himself, don't you worry. Look!" And she tucked a jar of her own made apricot preserve under the white cloth. "That'll make up for the delay."

No Scipio. We even searched the chapel with a lantern in case he was lying injured, hit by flying glass in the melee, in some dark corner. Mr Drury went back to the print shop. Will and I said goodnight glumly. None of us dared voice the horrible thought that was in our minds. Scipio was missing. So was the treasure.

Chapter nine

GONE!

1794

Whence drew the enlighten'd Sage the moral plan,
 That man should ever be the friend of man;
 Should eye with tenderness all living forms,
 His brother-emmets, and his sister-worms.

(Erasmus Darwin, The Temple of Nature)

$\mathcal{N}$ow passed the most horrible time I can remember. The prospect of all that money had been before me for a very short time yet I had already begun to feel it was mine by right. I was devastated and numb with disappointment. Even when I managed, just for a moment, to remind myself that I was no worse off than before that avalanche of riches had tumbled out before our eyes, the thought that Scipio, my dear friend, had betrayed me plunged me into deeper despair than ever.

At first I was desperately hoping Scipio would turn up and the money, or at least knowledge of its whereabouts, with him. But night fell and there was no sign of him, no sign of the money. There was no going back either to the moment before that strange inheritance had been poured out in front of me.

That night I tossed and turned. Will and I had been pushing and pulling at the back of the drawer in a pointless effort to make the desk disgorge the treasure it no longer contained. Now I pummelled my mind but it too was empty of any solution to the puzzle. Where was Scipio? Where was the money? Had Scipio taken it? Why would he do something so base, so unlike him? It seemed impossible: he was so pleasant, so friendly; everyone in Derby loved him. Could we all have been horribly wrong? The whole matter was as impenetrable as the denser lines of the Doctor's poetry but I could not give up the struggle to find some meaning, some clue, some solution.

Between waking and sleeping the need to find Scipio merged with the need to find answers to those other questions that often bothered me when trying to sleep. I was filled with an uneasy feeling that I lacked more than one kind of knowledge that was essential to my peace of mind. I woke in the morning with a knotted feeling of misery in my stomach.

That day I went straight to Dr Darwin for help and he listened to the whole story with concern. I did not hide the extraordinary tale of the treasure from him and he agreed that it looked very bad for Scipio.

"I can't believe it of him, Sir," I said. "He was such a good friend."

The Doctor looked grave. "You know that no one c-could be a more s-sincere abolitionist than I," he said. "No one c-could abhor s-slavery more than I d-do. N-nevertheless – and I do not m-much speak of these findings s-since they would g-give f-fuel to those who op-p-ppose abolition – you will b-be aware that in that g-great chain of b-being that developed f-from the f-first living f-filament, the b-black or Negro occupies a lower or s-subordinate place to the white m-man. And that includes his m-moral p-perceptions."

Scipio's gentle but accusing words came at once to my mind, "The apes and monkeys, which developed into Africans like me and then, finally, the pinnacle of creation." The idea that he and I were not equals had revolted me then – and I found it still did, even now.

"Sir, why do you oppose slavery, if that is the case?" I asked.

"B-because we should have c-concern for *all* l-living things," he replied. "All vegetables and animals arose f-from a s-single b-beginning, a living p-point or f-fibre. W-we are all related. It is the exercise of s-sympathy which b-balances the m-misery of the w-world and so b-brings an equilibrium. But M-Matthew," he added, turning to more practical matters, "I think it w-would be w-wise if n-no one m-mentioned the d-discovery of the t-treasure; I will inform the m-magistrates – Mr Leaper m-might be b-best as he has c-connections with your chapel – that Scipio is m-missing and also a s-sum of m-money. They c-can order a s-search of the neighbourhood."

No trace of Scipio could be found that day despite Dr Darwin's enquiries. "It's no good," said Will, dejectedly. "We've got to face up to it. He's taken the treasure and gone."

We tried the desk yet again, of course, pushing and pulling to see if somehow there was some strange trick to it that had sealed up the valuables in yet another compartment but, no matter what we did, the desk would disgorge nothing but empty space.

I sat down on Mr Drury's chair. "I can't believe it," I said for the hundredth time. "We helped him. We looked after him when he was escaping. How can he have run off with ... with my money?"

Will was almost bitter. "I hate myself for saying it," he said, "but it is the only explanation. And it would not be the first time someone has disappointed their rescuer. You've heard of Mr Granville Sharp, haven't you, the abolition campaigner?"

I nodded. Everyone knew of him; he was probably the kindest person on earth. He had been so determined and successful in rescuing ex-slaves that were being illegally detained that the mere mention that he was interested in a case was often enough to get the captive released.

"Well, he once rescued a man from being forced back into slavery and got him a place in a party going to found a colony in West Africa. When this ex-slave got there do you know what he did?"

I shook my head.

"He joined up with the slave traders and started trading in slaves himself."

Surely this was disheartening enough, I thought, to put Will off his enthusiasm for the abolition campaign. "But you still back abolition, write about it in the paper and so on?" I asked.

Like Dr Darwin, Will had a reason for carrying on with the cause but it was different to the Doctor's – quite the opposite, in fact.

"Oh yes," he said. "Mr Archer put it well, I think, in that sermon about the soul of a Hindu or an African being the same as ours. God created us, all of us. Adam was made in His image, and we are Adam's descendants whatever the colour of our skin. We are sinful but we are not just animals. That's why I like Agard Street. Abolition makes sense when you see it the way they do. Granville Sharp hasn't given up and neither shall I!"

"Good for you," I said suddenly as a new hope sprang up in me, "and I won't give up on Scipio either! I don't know what has happened to him but I'm determined to find out and I'm sure he's innocent. Whoever took my money it was not him."

Will smiled. "And I hope you are right," he said. "Whatever has happened though, we'll do everything we can to find him even if we have to turn Derby upside down!"

In the kitchen Mrs B confronted me. "Disappeared, hasn't he, that Scipio? I told young Susan, I said to her, 'If he's just gone off and left you like that he's not worth crying over. Just because he's got a fancy way of talking ...'"

Although I wanted to defend my late friend I had no arguments, no ammunition. It was just my emotions against hard facts and Mrs B continued, "There was a rough-looking man asking for him in the market place yesterday, you know, a stranger. One of his old associates, I dare say."

"A stranger?" I remembered the circumstances of Scipio's arrival among us and I clutched at this sudden straw. "Did you speak to him, Mrs B?"

"Not I," she said indignantly. "I'd not speak to such a ruffian. Someone else told him to go to Drury's, the printer's shop, but I did hear his name. A younger fellow with him, nasty looking he was too, called him ... now what was it ... I remember thinking it was the name of that wicked king in the Bible ... Ahab ... no not that one ... now who was it ...?"

"Herrod," I said quietly.

"Yes," she answered in surprise. "That was it. Herrod."

I clung to the straw with all my might. "Is Dr Darwin in his study, do you know, Mrs B?"

"I could ask the m-magistrates for a w-warrant – *Habeas Corpus*," said the Doctor when I had made my explanations, "but I would n-not be able to g-get one unless I knew the n-name *and* the p-place where Scipio is b-being held. Without that knowledge a w-warrant w-would be of n-no use in any case. Go down to the m-market, M-Matthew, n-now, and m-make some enquiries – s-see if anyone remembers this f-fellow Herrod or knows him. I'll see to the d-dispensary. I am on d-duty there m-myself this afternoon in any c-case."

I set off for the market which was in full swing that morning under a sky leaden with the threat of snow. The women clutched their shawls round them as they hurried to make their purchases; the air was raw. I could have had potatoes, poultry, butter, Derby cheese, apples, cabbages for the asking but news of the sinister Mr Herrod was less easy to come by. I was determined to find information, if there was any at all to be had, and I made enquiries systematically at every stall.

"Yes, Young Sir," said the apple woman politely. "Oh yes. Plenty of strangers – and some the worse for drink in the afternoon. I took myself home early. 'You come home if there's trouble', that's what my husband says. I didn't like the look of it, Sir, and I thought they'd be a thieving set of rascals. Herrod, Sir? No, I can't say I heard the name."

I made my way stall by weary stall with no success and was thinking dejectedly of going back to Full Street when someone pulled at my coat. I looked down to find a ragged urchin looking up at me.

"Sir," he said, "weren't you asking about the man who was looking for Mr Africanus yesterday?"

"Yes!" I said eagerly. "Can you tell me anything about him?"

"Yes, Sir, he spoke to my mother. She told him to go to the print shop and she sent me with him to show him the way, thinking he might give me something but he didn't. Just kicked me, Sir, when I asked if he could spare anything."

"Where is your mother now?" I asked looking round.

He led me to an ancient-looking dame who was hawking old clothes, brooms and other broken-down items near the edge of the market. She could offer no very coherent description of the man who had spoken to her but I thought the lad himself might have more to tell me. With the old woman's indifferent consent I took him to the back door of Mrs B's kitchen, thinking the warm atmosphere and a bite to eat might get the information I needed – whatever that was.

Mrs B bristled at first at the very sight of the lad in her neat, clean kitchen. But while I explained I was conducting researches on behalf of the Doctor, she cast an experienced eye over him, quickly decided his poverty was genuine and provided a stool near the fire and some good hot bread and milk.

"Can't be too careful, Matt," she explained out of the side of her mouth. "Don't want the house burgled by some ruffian who's sent him here to look round," and she shut the pantry door and turned the key as she spoke.

In between spoonfuls I gathered the meagre facts that were available. The man was short: he smelt of strong drink. He had told the lad to clear off once he had been shown the print shop. The lad had lingered, however, not having been paid, and had seen that the man had not attempted to enter the shop or knock at the door. Instead he had left his younger associate to wait for him and had gone down the side of the shop building, looking into each of the windows. More than that I could not discover except that the time, as far as the urchin could describe it, coincided with the time we had opened the desk and discovered the treasure. I remembered now that Scipio had immediately shuttered the window.

"You think Scipio was caught and taken away by his old master, then?" asked Will when I told him the results of my investigations. "Under cover of the rioting?"

"I'm sure of it," I answered. "Herrod obviously wanted his *property* back more than we all thought he did. Perhaps he even put off his voyage to Jamaica until he could get his hands on him again. We've got to find him, Will, before he's loaded on some vessel in Liverpool."

"I think you're right!" Will sounded relieved. "It makes much more sense than the idea of Scipio making off with the money. Herrod must have hung round the place looking for Scipio, saw him through the window perhaps and lingered to watch ... and then when the desk shot open ..."

"No one broke in but then Scipio had keys ..." Scipio's keys! They'd been used by his villainous old master to open up the shop while we were all busy watching the riot develop. It made me shudder as I thought about it.

"Mr Drury's been making some quiet enquiries," said Will, "as well as getting all our locks changed here. As far as he can find out, no one has tried to sell any of that jewellery here in Derby, at least not yet."

"It's not likely Herrod would try to sell it so soon or here in Derby," I said. "He's not to know I couldn't identify any of it."

It was a bitter thought. How much I had managed to build on that brief glimpse of riches! All that remained now was the little crescent moon in my pocket, its very shape a cruel mockery of my dashed hopes for the future.

"I think he'd be more likely to get moving straight for Liverpool and take the whole of your fortune with him to Jamaica. It would be very easy to get rid of it there: no one would know and no one would ask questions. We should be asking Mr Campion at the Bell Inn who left on the coach." said Will. "Where would they go to from here to pick up the London to Liverpool stage?"

"They'd never manage to get Scipio into a stagecoach against his will without anyone noticing!" I replied. "No, they must have thought of some other way if they are heading for Liverpool. Maybe they are hiding him somewhere in Derby until we stop looking for him. Or what if they have their own coach?"

"They don't sound like the types to own a coach of their own but in any case that would have to be put up at the Bell too," said Will, "I'll go and see what I can find out."

Will's researches with the post-boys at the George and ostlers at the Bell drew an absolute blank, as I had feared they would. I went home to Full Street, weary and frustrated. Dr Darwin was out. I wrote a short report of what little I had been able to find out and left it on his desk in case he should go into his study on his return. I was about to make my way to the kitchen in search of something to eat when I suddenly remembered that Scipio had swum the Derwent to get to the chapel on the night we first found him. That meant that Herrod had an accomplice somewhere on the opposite bank! If he was being hidden we should concentrate our search there. We would have to be careful though. Suppose we found him and could not rescue him ourselves? Suppose we needed a warrant?

If Herrod and his friend got wind of what we were up to, by the time Dr Darwin had got a warrant they would have moved Scipio elsewhere. I was angry with myself that I had not thought of searching the east bank of the river before and I hurried off to find Will.

I knocked on the side door of the print shop. Will let me in and I explained my idea.

"What should we do?" he queried, bending down to pick up a slip of paper from the floor. "If we go asking people whether they've seen a captive or know anything about it, a warrant will be a waste of time – Herrod and his crony – or cronies – will just get out and imprison Scipio elsewhere."

"Well I think we should take great care and just begin by snooping around. There are a couple of barns beyond the Doctor's orchards for instance and ..."

Will was not listening. He was staring at the piece of paper he had just picked up. "Look at this, Matt!" he exclaimed. "Someone knows where Herrod is alright!"

Chapter ten

THE PURSUIT OF THE *ROBERT*

1794

GNOMES! as you now dissect with hammers fine
The granite-rock, the nodul'd flint calcine;
Grind with strong arm, the circling chertz betwixt,
Your pure Ka-o-lins and Pe-tun-tses mixt;
O'er each red saggars burning cave preside,
The keen-eyed Fire-Nymphs blazing by your side;
And pleased on WEDGWOOD ray your partial smile,
A new Etruria decks Britannia's isle.

*(Erasmus Darwin, The Botanic Garden.
Part I: The Economy of Vegetation)*

*W*ill handed me the piece of paper. It was a small printed form, filled out in a neat clerical hand. It was headed with the words, "Shipped on board James Renshaw and Co's boat *Robert*. Swarkestone for Harecastle" and dated 14th January 1794. Below this was a handwritten list of goods: cheeses, barrels, casks, sundries ... with the tonnage of each. In a space marked "Steerer" was written, "Jacob Herrod."

"Where's this come from?"

"Someone's pushed it under the door ... "

"Who? ... Someone who wanted to give you a hint about Herrod? That he, no it must be his brother or some other relative, was a canal boatman ... but how would they know ... how would they get hold of this? ... The fourteenth was the day before yesterday ... before the meeting ..."

I turned the paper over. On the back were some large black marks that looked as though someone had made them with a burnt stick or a piece of coal; a twisted shape and a badly made triangle ... or the letters S, A.

"Scipio!" I felt suddenly jubilant. "He's on the canal ... in that boat! He's scrawled his initials on the back, look!"

"Matt," said Will urgently, "take it to Doctor Darwin, quickly. He'll know what to do if it's anything to do with the Grand Trunk Canal. Why, there would not *be* a Grand Trunk Canal if it were not for him! Is he in?"

I rushed back to Full Street clutching the paper and almost burst into the Doctor's study.

"It's a w-waybill," he said after listening to my breathless explanations, and pulling out a book from the case beside his writing desk, he opened it and folded out a long thin map.

"Here is the n-navigation," he explained, smoothing out the map of the canal, on the construction of which he had had so much influence. "If Scipio's abductors t-took him – in a c-cart s-say– to S-Stenson's L-Lock," he pointed, "or even b-back to S-Swarkestone L-Lock," his chubby finger marked the place again, "he c-could have been p-put on a n-narrow-boat in the d-dark and no one would b-be any the w-wiser."

"They could get him to Liverpool then, couldn't they, Sir?"

"They c-could," said the Doctor, "via the M-Mersey though they will have to t-transfer him onto the B-Bridgwater Navigation to Runcorn at P-Preston B-Brook and then onto a M-Mersey flat for the t-trip down the M-Mersey itself. This waybill – you s-say it was p-pushed under the s-side d-door at the *M-Mercury* office – I s-suppose it m-must have been s-somehow p-passed by Scipio himself to s-someone on a b-boat going in the opposite d-direction. Whoever received it m-must have b-been asked to hand it over in turn to s-someone who could d-deliver it."

"You mean he got hold of the waybill somehow and managed to attract someone's attention ..."

The Doctor examined the marks on the reverse of the paper again. "I think he was restricted in his m-movements – perhaps his hands t-tied or in m-manacles of the type used by s-slave t-traders – when he wrote these c-crude characters." He returned to the map. "Etruria is the k-key. The p-passage of n-narrow-boats along the c-canal varies in speed d-depending on how m-many locks have to be p-passed and so on. Even if the b-boat was kept under way through every minute of d-daylight it c-could not reach Etruria b-before ..." he hesitated, "... b-before late on Friday (if it got under w-way at f-first light this m-morning) at the earliest – n-not until S-Saturday p-perhaps if there is a d-delay at any of the wharfs. The loss of this b-bill itself may d-delay the b-boat and perhaps even p-prevent it p-passing the wharf at Haywood J-Junction, j-just here." He pointed to the map again.

"Etruria, Sir?" I asked, looking at the map. "Why is that the key?"

"I have a f-friend at Etruria," smiled the Doctor, "a very g-good f-friend."And with that he sat down at his writing desk and began a letter: "My dear Wedgwood, Please excuse this hasty scrawl ..."

Doctor Darwin may have been a bulky person but he could move with speed when he needed to and he was an expert organiser. Ruling out the post from the George Inn as far too slow he had Edward, the gardener's lad, riding off with the letter at once to the home of the famous pottery manufacturer, Mr Wedgwood, some thirty miles distant. Wedgwood himself was as intimately connected with the development of the canal as the Doctor. One of its main purposes was to carry materials into his Etruria works and his finished china and pottery wares to Liverpool and Hull. "Mr Wedgwood c-can have the *R-Robert* stopped at Etruria," said the Doctor. "I've given him s-sufficient information to g-get a w-warrant issued by a m-magistrate ready for when the b-boat arrives. It is a full m-moon tonight and a c-clear sky so young Edward should have n-no t-trouble."

He then went straight to Mr Leaper's house for a warrant himself, telling me to fetch Will Ward quickly. On the way out he ordered a wallet of bread and cheese for us from a startled Mrs B in the kitchen.

Mr Drury was happy for Will to go when he heard what was afoot. In what seemed like no time we were bowling along the Lichfield turnpike, squeezed together in the Doctor's own special carriage, clutching our bread and cheese and dashing round the corners at what seemed like a terrifying speed. The doctor was calm: he had designed the steering system of his carriage himself and considered it incapable of being upset. Nor was he worried as night began to fall. For years he had been journeying along this very road in this carriage to meetings of the Lunar Society. After a good dinner and plenty of scientific discussion, he would go rushing home again in his carriage by moonlight.

"I think your b-best plan would be to follow the t-towpath as fast as you can to b-begin with. I will speak to the Cheque Clerk at Fradley J-Junction; he will b-be able to tell us if the *R-Robert* has b-been through and h-how l-long ago."

At Fradley Junction all was in darkness but the Doctor rapped on the door of the cottage by the wharf and the Cheque Clerk himself opened the door. At first he seemed a little impatient at being roused from his fireside for the Doctor's stammer meant he could never explain anything quickly. But the sight of the magistrate's warrant frightened him into action and he led us at once to his office and lighted an oil lamp. We found ourselves in a complete library of bound volumes of past waybills, toll books, ledgers as well as great spikes holding stacks of duplicated receipts where the earthy smell of the leather book-binding mingled with a whiff of lamp oil. The lamplight wavered in the draught from the open door as the Cheque Clerk began thumbing his way rapidly back through the current ledger to find the entry for the *Robert*.

"Here it is, Sir," he said turning the great book round for the Doctor to read, "'James Renshaw and Co.'s *Robert*. Swarkestone for Harecastle with barrels, cheeses and sundries then empty to Etruria wharf.' They'll be loading pottery ware there for Liverpool and go via the Bridgwater canal at Preston Brook to Runcorn, I should think."

"When did they p-pass here?" asked the Doctor. "Ah y-yes, I can s-see f-from the entry: half p-past one this afternoon. They are hours ah-head."

"Where can we get horses?" asked Will.

"I'm af-fraid you'll have t-to walk," replied the Doctor before the Cheque Clerk, plainly horrified at this suggestion, could answer. "Riding along the t-tow path is strictly f-forbidden by the c-company for the very g-good reason that it would be extremely d-dangerous!"

"Walk!" I exclaimed. "However will we catch up with a moving boat on foot?"

"It won't b-be hard. The *Robert* will b-be slowed d-down by every l-lock," explained the Doctor. "Mr W-Wedgwood was t-telling me j-just recently about the queues of b-boats waiting to p-pass through the locks at b-busy t-times. They will also have to t-tie up after d-dark. They will not g-get moving again until it is d-daylight. You, however, c-can set off well b-before first light *and* g-get a g-good n-night's sleep."

I could see Will was sick with disappointment. He had fully expected to go haring off in the dark along the towpath on horseback! "Sleep!" he exclaimed.

"Yes, s-sleep!" reiterated the Doctor, quite sternly. "You will n-need it. The p-power of volition is t-totally s-suspended during s-sleep – and M-Matthew will b-be able t-to tell you why that m-means it is important while you get your s-supper at the S-Swan!"

Will and I set off along the towpath well before first light, having spent the night at the inn. I can testify that Will had snored away as soon as his head hit the pillow despite his protesting that he would not be able to sleep a wink until we had rescued Scipio!

"Have you got the warrant safe?" I asked anxiously in the thick darkness while Will fumbled about with the lantern he had managed to borrow from the inn.

He patted his pocket for answer, adding, "and the Doctor's written instructions about detailed searches and what to do when we reach Haywood Junction and so on."

"As soon as a walking surveyor passes I'll alert him, Sirs," the Cheque Clerk had assured us. These men were the canal company's officials. They policed the boats to ensure there was no pilfering of goods and to report needed repairs of the canal itself. "I'll make a full report in the records here," he had added.

The morning was still horribly dark and we picked out our uncertain way. The growing daylight gradually improved matters and after a while we no longer needed the light of the lantern. It became clear, too, that there were good reasons for the Trent and Mersey Canal Company's rules which prevented us riding along the towpath.

"We couldn't really have just thundered along at a gallop until we reached this junction place, could we?" said Will, ruefully admitting the wisdom of the regulations, as we picked our way along the cindered path by the water's edge. I could sense his frustration: we were only plodding and he was thirsting for a high speed chase that would bring us to Scipio's rescue.

Alas, it is not a simple matter to use a canal towpath even in daylight, especially for anyone not used to it. Once it is daylight the path becomes a highway for horses travelling in either direction. Each horse is attached by a line to the boat it is drawing. The steerers had perfected the tricky art of passing each other with minimal delay. We watched in amazement as what seemed to our inexperienced eyes an inevitable collision began to develop. But no! The tow rope of one boat was simply allowed to sink into the water to allow the other boat to pass over it, the horse neatly stepping over the length of rope on the towpath without a pause.

But for the inexperienced walker on the towpath it was another matter. The boats were not going to relax their steady pace for us. The steerers had a living to earn and we were a nuisance. "Watch out!" I cried to Will for the twentieth time as he strode confidently on towards an oncoming horse. If he wasn't more careful, I was sure he would end up in some gruesome accident with a tow line that would see him flung into the water – and perhaps even crushed between the bank and an oncoming boat.

And now we began to make enquiries, calling at wharf offices and lock-keepers' cottages. We found that, despite these continual halts, every time we had news of the *Robert* we were inching closer to her. However, it was slow work. When we arrived at Handsacre the sun, though invisible through the mist and drizzle, must have been well up. We discovered from the wharfinger's recollections that the *Robert* had passed through just before nightfall the previous afternoon. "We're gaining on her!" said Will jubilantly, adding, "There is a tunnel ahead; perhaps that's slowed her down too."

We pressed on into the cold and dreary damp. A heavy sky reflected grey in the water. We passed two boats, but could get no news of the *Robert* from either of them. I peered into the tunnel mouth at Armitage as I waited for Will who had walked back again talking to the steerer of a boat that emerged. A kind of grey steam rose eerily off the water. Beyond it nothing was visible. The towpath led on into the unknown. I shuddered, hesitant to step into the yawning murk of the tunnel mouth even to shelter from the drizzle. I wondered how long this tunnel might be but peering into the gloom gave me no clue. We could have miles to go, I thought, and I was beginning to feel footsore.

Then suddenly Will turned and practically ran towards me. "We've got her!" he shouted triumphantly. "She's tied up on the other side of the tunnel. We are in luck! Their horse has cast a shoe! One of them's had to go off to a smithy with the horse." And without a word of explanation he plunged into the eerie gloom leaving me to follow, wondering what on earth would happen now.

The steerer's report seemed accurate and as we emerged from the tunnel we could see a boat tied up by the towpath. When we came up with it I made out the first three letters of the name *Robert* painted on the side just visible above the tall frost-blackened weeds at the water's edge.

"What shall we do now?" I whispered but Will was confident. "We get on board and get Scipio out of it, of course, come on!" and before I could ask what our plan of action might be, he was clambering onto the boat and hammering on the door of the cabin.

Chapter eleven

COLWICH

1794

So with strong arm immortal BRINDLEY leads
His long canals, and parts the velvet meads;
Winding in lucid lines, the watery mass
Mines the firm rock, or loads the deep morass,
With rising locks a thousand hills alarms,
Flings o'er a thousand streams its silver arms,
Feeds the long vale, the nodding woodland laves,
And Plenty, Arts, and Commerce freight the waves.

(Erasmus Darwin. The Botanic Garden. Part I.)

"*A*re you the steerer of this boat?"

"I might be. Who are you?"

"I have a warrant to search for someone who is illegally imprisoned here and to search for stolen goods!"

"Well, have you now?" The tone was quiet and menacing. The man was small but stocky and he moved quickly to bar Will's way. "Well you're not coming in my cabin whatever you've got or whoever you think might be on board. As for stolen goods – you leave that to the company's surveyors and mind your own business." As he spoke I noticed him glancing along the towpath in a way that made me turn and look in that direction. A man was leading a horse along the path towards the boat, a big man, tall and broad with a beefy look. Already! There must be a smithy nearby. "Get off this boat now before I have you in the canal, Mister, and take your precious warrant with you while it is still dry," said the man aboard the boat. He spoke softly but the tone had a grim determination in it. He took a step towards Will and suddenly raised his voice to shout, "Tom!" The man and horse at once quickened their pace. "You get off this boat," he reiterated to Will, "or I'll get you off and it won't be pretty. Tom! Tom!"

"I'm not leaving here until I've got Scipio," said Will desperately. "Let me pass. I've a warrant from the magistrate," and he made towards the cabin doorway, knocking into the tiller as he did so. The movement swayed the boat slightly and her name showed briefly above the weeds that had obscured it. In horror I read it in full: *Robin.*

"Will!" I shouted urgently. "Will, stop! It's the wrong boat it's not the *Robert* at all – oh stop!"

By this time the man with the horse had arrived. He took in the situation and grabbed me roughly by the collar. "'Ere!" he demanded of Will, "What you doing? Don't you mess with my boat! You get off now or I throw your pal in too." He dragged me forcefully towards the brink.

"Will!" I shouted again, "Get off quickly, I tell you it's not the *Robert!*"

The explanations were not pleasant and took some time. The boatmen were angry and suspicious and the sight of the warrant helped but little for only the big man with the horse could actually read enough to recognise what it was. I'd escaped the ducking but only just.

Will was crestfallen as we trudged along the towpath – at first. But gradually his optimism returned. He was soon expecting once more to find, if not the *Robert* herself, at least the vital clue that would lead us to Scipio round every bend of the canal. I was becoming less sanguine. The episode with the *Robin* had left me shaken. There were so many boats, it was like looking for a needle in a watery haystack and it began to seem a hopeless task. We crossed the Trent, for the navigation strides boldly over the river at this point on a mighty aqueduct. At another time I would have enjoyed this sensation but cold, wet, weariness and worry took away any pleasure I might have had in this ingenious crossing of water by water. We tried to quicken our pace towards the lock we knew was ahead but I knew we were not matching the speed we had adopted at our outset.

"What's happening up there?" asked Will suddenly, pointing ahead. A knot of people was gathered on the bank and Will broke into a run. "C'mon Matt! This might be what we're looking for." I began running too, my weariness forgotten. Was it the *Robert* at last? Had someone discovered Scipio?

My drooping spirits lifted at the thought.

Despite our burst of speed the crisis at the lock was more or less over by the time we reached the scene and again we were doomed to disappointment. A small boy was being simultaneously scolded and carried indoors by the lock-keeper's wife while various on-lookers offered helpful advice such as, "Can't someone fetch 'is mother?" and "Get 'im inside 'fore 'e freezes," or "What 'e needs is a drop o' something warming."

"Went in after his dog, the little fool!" explained the clearly shaken lock-keeper in answer to our enquiries. "Lucky for him I closed the sluices – just in time too – otherwise he'd be dead. Had to fish him out myself. Dog came to no harm but the stupid child nearly drowned. I've send my daughter off to fetch his mother. *Robert?* Yes, maybe ... early this morning? Could have been ... Herrod? No, don't know the name, Sirs."

We trudged on disappointed again. Even Will was more subdued. The drizzle now began to change into something worse. A steady downpour of freezing rain began to fall in an unrelenting torrent.

Both of us were strong walkers but after a while the wet began to penetrate our clothing. Soon our boots were squelching and damp wool was beginning to chafe our legs and ankles, slowing us down even more. We no longer asked anyone about the boat we were seeking but concentrated all our efforts on keeping on the path and out of the canal ourselves, our heads down and water trickling off the very brims of our hats. It was well past dinner time when we arrived at the toll office at Haywood Junction, wet through, cold despite the effort of walking, dispirited and feeling that the elusive *Robert* was no longer within our grasp.

Flickering firelight glimmered through the toll window at Haywood Junction and peering in was like looking at an unattainable picture of warmth and comfort. The Cheque Clerk took one look at the now damp warrant and beckoned us into his little office where a bright fire was blazing.

"You just stand there and get yourselves dry," he said. "Henry! Where are you, lad? Come and make up the fire for the gentlemen."

We stood steaming in front of the grateful warmth while he bustled about organising Henry – a "lad" who looked to be about ninety and rather slow moving when he appeared – and I don't think I've ever enjoyed the comfort of a cheerful fire so much.

When we explained about the *Robert,* he reached down a ledger, and pointed to an entry. "Twenty after ten this morning, Sirs. They had no waybill," he explained. "Very irregular. First they tried to show me a copy of an old bill that was out of date and *then* they admitted they'd lost it somehow. I know Jake Herrod, of course, not someone whose word would stand very high, if you know what I mean, Sirs. And he had his brother with him too. Ugly looking character though he could speak fair. Not a man who knows anything about the boats on the navigation, I'd have said." He paused meaningfully and then continued, "I went over the whole boat assessing what they had loaded onboard and then I gauged it."

"What about the waybill?" asked Will. "Did you issue some kind of duplicate?"

"I made out a temporary waybill, Sir, and reserved a copy here, for confirmation of the exact weights from the last wharf they passed if it became necessary. Then I let them go on. James Renshaw and Company are a reputable firm and they have an account. I told them I would have to make a special entry in the ledger adjusting the tonnages when I had seen the record from the previous wharf and that it would show on Renshaw's account. I had to make an extra charge to Renshaw and Co. too. They had no choice but to accept that."

"We know where that lost waybill is," Will explained. "That's how we come to be here with our warrant in the first place." And he explained the whole story to the astonished Cheque Clerk. "So we are looking for an African man, possibly injured," he concluded. "Could anyone have been hidden on the boat?"

The Cheque Clerk was positive. "No, Sir," he said definitely. "I went over the whole cargo – every inch of the boat – had the cloths off – there was no one on board except the Herrod brothers."

"What about the cabin?" asked Will, "Could someone have been hidden in there?"

"I went into the cabin as it happens, Sir," he replied. "I put my head in just to look around for the waybill itself – thinking it might have been mislaid. To find it would have saved a deal of work. As I said to Jake Herrod, two pairs of eyes are better than one when it comes to something lost. But it was not there – at least I could not see it – and a narrow boat cabin is not not much of a place, Sir."

The kindly Cheque Clerk went off to find us something to eat but I could not really think about food. Scipio was not on the boat! Our brains were whirling as we steamed away by the fire trying to piece together what had happened on board the *Robert*. My mind went back to the incident at Colwich Lock. Suppose Scipio had tried to make an escape – and drowned in the process. "No!" said Will firmly when I voiced the thought. "No! He swam the Derwent, remember, a canal is nothing compared to that. Don't you worry, Scipio will take some stopping!" This was true – and heartening – but then I remembered Dr Darwin remarking that Scipio's hands might be manacled. I shuddered, thinking of the icy water and a man with his hands bound together in iron.

At some point we knew Scipio had got hold of the waybill and managed to pass it to someone – presumably on a boat going in the opposite direction – with instructions to get it to the *Mercury* Office in Derby. But when had one of the Herrods noticed the waybill was missing? Perhaps not for some time.

"When they found the waybill was gone they must have realised the boat would be inspected thoroughly at the next wharf," said Will. "That would be the end for them if they did not get rid of Scipio first. But who knows when that was?"

"But they had gone to all that trouble to capture him," I said bewildered. "If they dumped him now, why even stay on the canal themselves? There are quicker ways to get to Liverpool, unencumbered."

"But they *are* encumbered!" said Will, "Because they've got your money! Maybe they came to Derby with the object of getting hold of Scipio but now they've got something much more valuable than a recaptured slave. On a canal boat they could hide it with no questions asked. Travelling on the road they would have endless difficulties transporting something heavy and yet quite small without it being obvious to all and sundry that it contained valuables. They would be vulnerable at every inn! And anyone who found out what two rogues like that were carrying would be suspicious – to say nothing of highwaymen and the rest."

The money! The hunt for Scipio had been so intense that I had almost forgotten it. Then it struck me that to "get rid of" Scipio might well mean killing him. How else could they stop him giving them away? The thought that the sum of money I possessed was so huge that a thief was prepared to kill my friend to get hold of it chilled me more than the air of the grey winter evening had done. I voiced my horror. "Have they killed him, Will?"

"They'll hang if they have! We'll make sure of that." Will was suddenly grim and his hand went to the warrant in his pocket.

"They can't be far ahead of us, if they passed here at twenty past ten," I said. "What's the time now?"

"It can't be much after three," said Will. "Look, we must go after them *and* we must go back to find out what's happened to Scipio; we'll have to split up. I'll go straight on; you go back. I can walk on and come up with them if they are tied up somewhere."

The mistake with the *Robin* had been salutary. From the very beginning of this adventure I had wondered what would happen when we actually came on the *Robert*. Using the warrant, I thought we would need to summon some local aid before trying to board the boat or challenge the villains. The resistance offered by the innocent boatmen of the *Robin* proved that my supposition was far from groundless. Unlike them, the Herrods would be desperate men. The idea of Will, alone, in the gathering dark and on foot, confronting them was unendurable. They were the men who somehow had trapped Scipio and then – who knows? – perhaps even murdered him; they would not scruple to dispose of Will.

"No!" I said, "Not on your own, Will. It's too dangerous."

"I can't go on not knowing what's happened!" fumed Will. "And what's more I don't believe you could either – not knowing whether Scipio is alive or dead!"

He was right, of course. "No," I said again. "Of course not, but there is no danger in going back alone, only in going on."

"Well, what about getting some help? The Cheque Clerk must know where we can find a magistrate, a constable or someone."

At this point, right on cue, that helpful official reappeared with a tray of cold dinner, fetched from the inn by the "lad". Will asked him if a magistrate or constable could be found.

The man looked grave. "You could go over to the Hall and show your warrant to Mr Anson, the magistrate, if he's at home. He may help you – perhaps send some men to go with you. Or he may advise you to ride straight on the Etruria and if so, Sirs, I would take his advice. I can send the lad with you up to the Hall to show you the way."

I ate my cold food as quickly as I could. I don't think Will even noticed what he was eating, he was so eager to be off. The "lad" was summoned and away they went to the Hall on a couple of horses from the nearby inn, leaving me to retrace our steps in an effort to find out what had become of Scipio.

I was full of foreboding as to what I might discover as I tramped along and very uncertain as to how I would discover it. I had dried out pretty much. The rain had stopped now and darkness began to close in. Then a bright moon arose and the temperature dropped sharply as the sky cleared. A guttering lantern was all I had for company. I had insisted that the other "lad" (only marginally junior to the first) remain to assist Will, in case, should he return to carry on up the towpath, his party needed more numbers. Every time I recalled what had happened – or nearly happened – at our encounter with the *Robin* I became more convinced that I was right to insist Will did not carry on alone. The darkness deepened and the cold increased. My pace was slow and I swung my lantern over the black dismal water of the canal as I retraced my route, peering at its still surface. There was not a breath of wind now to ripple the water or stir the bare branches of the trees. A deep, chill silence settled round me; there was no sound but the crunching of my own footsteps on the gravelly path. I dreaded to admit to myself that

I was searching the murky surface of the canal for the body of my friend.

I had tramped what felt like miles in this way with nothing but my unquiet thoughts to accompany me when, peering into the moonlit gloom ahead, I discerned a light bobbing along the towpath towards me. As I approached a voice hailed me, "'Ay up there! Be that t'doctor?"

I hurried towards the speaker. "Can I help?" I asked when I was within proper speaking distance. "I am not a doctor but I have some medical training. Is someone ill?"

The man lifted up his lantern. By its light I saw a middle-aged man, a farmer I judged, of quite prosperous appearance, in leather gaiters and strong boots. His honest, round face was distorted with anxiety as he scrutinised me.

"Well aye, in a manner o' speaking," he replied. "Can'st come? 'E's like to die else, to my mind."

"Of course, I'll come," I said at once. "What is the matter? What has happened?"

"Thank ye kindly!" he sounded relieved. "As to what's 'appened I'm not rightly sure … but come this way; you can see for yoursel'." And lowering his lantern he stumped off along the path, beckoning to me to follow.

I could now see that the farmer had come from one of those small bridges that carry a country lane across the canal. He led me with great ungainly strides up onto the lane, across the bridge and though a farmyard to the door of the farmhouse. "Ellen," he called, as we entered, "I've got a doctor fer 'im."

I was just explaining that I was not technically a doctor when a light footstep sounded on the stairs and a neat-looking girl in a clean white apron appeared. When she saw me she looked puzzled.

"Where is Dr Trim ...?" she said. "That is ... Father, didn't you send for ...?"

"No," I explained hastily, "I'm not a doctor – just someone with some medical training. I'm assistant to Dr Erasmus Darwin of Derby and as I happened to be walking along the towpath I offered to help."

"Oh, thank you so much," she said. "Can you come up? We all think the poor man is dying and we don't know what to do ..."

I followed her up the stairs. "What has happened?" I asked again. "Has there been an accident?"

"Not an accident, well, there might have been, we don't know. Father just found him lying in the grass on the outside bank opposite the towpath. On his way to the the Methodist class meeting at dinner time he was – just by the bridge. This way please." And she opened a door and ushered me in.

Sitting in a chair beside the bed was an old dame in a white apron and cap who seemed to be asleep. On the bed, black and motionless with his hands manacled at the wrists, lay Scipio.

Chapter twelve

I AM NOT A DOCTOR

1794

But war, and pestilence, disease, and dearth,
Sweep the superfluous myriads from the earth.
Thus while new forms reviving tribes acquire
Each passing moment, as the old expire;
Like insects swarming in the noontide bower,
Rise into being, and exist an hour ...

(Erasmus Darwin, The Temple of Nature)

Scipio was suffering from the effects of extreme cold and wet. I took these things in at a glance and felt his pulse: it was steady and strong. On examination his left arm appeared to be broken.

"Can you have the fire built up in here?" I asked the girl, for the room was not particularly warm. "And is there a smith who can strike off this thing?" I pointed to the iron manacle. "He'll need a surgeon or a bone-setter to deal with that arm, not a doctor. How long has he been here in this state?"

I sounded exactly like a proper medical man and even as I said the words I felt so pleased, despite everything, at my own professionalism. I had pushed down my joy at finding Scipio alive and my burning desire to find out what had happened to him, allowing a smooth medical efficiency to take over which I was gratified to find I possessed.

"Well, it would be a little before noon when Father and the farm hands brought him in, I suppose," she replied, "I'm not quite sure of the time," and then turning to the dozy old woman, "Annie, dear, stir yourself! The doctor wants the fire built up."

The old dame staggered to her feet and tottered downstairs for more firewood.

"Do you have any spirits?" I asked the girl, abandoning any attempt to correct yet again the delightful misapprehension that I was a doctor. "The poor fellow has had a shock and needs to be revived and warmed."

Scipio had a strong constitution. Warmth and brandy had a good effect but I insisted he be kept quiet and not allowed to try to talk. A smith and a surgeon were probably not going to be available at that late hour so I made him as comfortable as I could, propping his manacled wrists on a pillow. The girl brought some harmless cordial of her own concoction that would come in handy if Scipio woke in the night and needed something soothing. Dismissing the old dame, I prepared to sit up with him through the night. Resisting for the time being the understandable curiosity of the farmer and his daughter, I told them only that I had been on the towpath for the very purpose of finding the man they had so kindly helped. I assured them I would explain all the details as soon as I could do so without exciting the patient.

"Answer to prayer, thee coming along t'cut like that, doctor," said the farmer, "Billy's just come home saying he can't find Dr Trim nowhere. If you're sure you're 'appy to sit up wi' 'im we'll away to bed for t'night – it's getting to be late, as you might say, now." And with that he closed the door – none too gently – before I had a chance to thank him for his kindness to my friend.

Scipio seemed now to be sleeping quietly and I sat beside him going through the day's events and trying to piece together in my mind what had happened. The room was really warm now, which was what Scipio needed, and I made up the fire and then settled down to watch him by its flickering light. The old dame's chair was comfortable and I was suddenly very weary. I must have fallen into a doze despite my resolution to keep watch for I woke with a start at the sound of my name.

"Matt? Matt! Where am I? What's happened?"

I sprang to life at once. "Scipio," I kept my voice low and calm, "just rest now; everything is fine. Don't try to talk. Just rest." And I put my hand on his brow to check for fever.

"I am resting, Matt," he said, his voice level again now. "Resting in Jesus ... It is all joy to know Him ... nothing can harm us, His children ..."

I knew that Scipio needed to be kept calm. I knew I should make some soothing remark and encourage him to sleep. So far my new-found professionalism had not deserted me despite my exhaustion and the stresses and strains of the last few days. But those words "... to know Him" seemed to stab into my worn-out heart and my inner strength failed completely. Whatever those words meant, and I had puzzled long over them, I knew they did not apply to me. I did not "know Him" of that I was certain. I looked at Scipio lying there, his manacled hands resting on the cushion, and he was smiling. His face had a quiet radiance that amazed me. Something seemed to snap inside me and I covered my face with my hands.

"How can I know Him?" I groaned, "How? I don't even understand what it *means* to know Him."

I looked up. Scipio's smile had dimmed and he looked very serious. "Matt," he said earnestly, "this is important! You need a Saviour – just as I did. You must seek Him and seek Him now: tomorrow may be too late."

"I don't know how to do so!" I said bitterly. "How can I seek Him whom I do not know?" My mind went back to that sermon by Mr Archer on the day we heard the news of

Monsieur Rabaut's death. The astounding events that had happened since, the riot and the robbery to say nothing of the chase after the *Robert,* had pushed it to the back of my mind but now his words returned with a new force.

"I cannot find Him for you," said Scipio, "You must ask Him yourself. Pray, Matt, pray!"

He was raising himself up from the supporting pillows and my professionalism reasserted itself. I was afraid that he would do some damage if he moved the broken arm – to say nothing of the pain.

"Lie down gently, Scipio," I said. "We'll get a surgeon to look at that break tomorrow but for now you must only rest." I settled him down again, smoothed the pillows and listened to his regular breathing as he closed his eyes again. But I did not close my own eyes. I did not dare to do so for fear I should fall asleep again. With my eyes open and fixed on Scipio's peaceful face I prayed, "Lord, please help me to find You. I know *about* Christ. But I simply don't know ..." What was it Mr Archer had said: "Examine yourselves? Christ must be in you, and you in Him?" The phrases came back to me but it was like a foreign language. I looked at Scipio. There was a world of difference between us and it had nothing to do with the colour of our skin.

The next morning was frosty, bright and clear. Dr Trim arrived: he too had been up all night with a patient. He was aptly named, a neat little man with a brisk but kindly professional manner.

"You have done the best thing possible, young man," he said to me, after examining Scipio, "and you look exhausted. When did you last have any sleep?"

By then I could not even remember clearly when or where I had last been to bed. The doctor laughed, though he must have been tired himself. "Get some rest then, or you'll be no help to the young African gentleman here. Samuel, is there anywhere on this farm the young man can have a sleep for a few hours? And can you send for a smith and a surgeon? That horrible iron thing must come off before the bone can be set – how one human being can put such a thing on another I do not know! It is proof of original sin if ever I saw it!"

Someone was shaking me very gently and calling, "Dr Batchelor, Dr Batchelor, Sir, the surgeon has come! Can you come up, please?"

The farmer's dainty daughter, Ellen, was looking down on me as I lay, boots and all, on a settle in the farmer's best parlour. I blinked for a moment. The surgeon? The surgeon – oh, Scipio – his arm – of course!

"Oh, I'm so sorry!" I gasped, rubbing my eyes, "Have I slept all day?"

"No, no," she smiled gently. "It is not yet noon and I'm sorry to waken you but the surgeon is asking to speak to you before he goes up.

The surgeon proved to be an efficient-looking fellow, brawny but with a kind face. "A clean break is it, Doctor? No fever?" he asked me as we went up the stairs.

"I'm afraid I'm not a doctor exactly," I began reluctantly, as Ellen showed us politely into the little front bedroom, "but there was no sign of fever when Dr Trim examined him this morning."

Scipio was lying as I had left him except that the manacle that had held his wrists was gone. The farmer must have got someone to remove it while I slept. He smiled at me as we entered the room. "The surgeon is here," I explained to him, "to look at your arm."

"Now then, old chap," said the surgeon talking to Scipio as one might to a child, "let's have a little look and see what you've done to yourself."

He took the arm up tenderly in his hands, one above and one below the point of the fracture as though to examine it with care. His movement was so gentle that Scipio scarcely winced. I bent towards him to watch, thinking I might learn from his method of examination. To my amazement, however, instead of a lengthy scanning of the arm he gazed at it for a moment and then without any warning, gave it a twisting wrench! Scipio screamed and then passed out but the surgeon calmly opened his bag and produced wooden splints and a sort of leather bandage with which he proceeded to strap up Scipio's arm, presumably to immobilise it in the correct position while the bone set. "Right," he said, as he worked, "that's got it into place. Now, does that lass have any smelling salts? And a drop o' brandy when he comes to? He'll have to keep it quite still until it's mended."

Scipio began to come round and the surgeon, satisfied, gave instructions that Dr Trim should see him again the following day and took his departure.

I felt Scipio's brow again and was pleased to find no fever. I sat with my friend for a couple of hours full of a quiet joy that he had been found and restored to me and that he was cleared of any hint of betrayal. I insisted on his keeping quiet and resolutely refused to let him talk or ask questions. He complained of no pain although I was sure the arm must be hurting.

A gentle knock at the door heralded Ellen with a bowl of oatmeal gruel. I fed Scipio with a spoon as a mother would feed a child and he took it patiently. Ellen also brought some sort of lotion concoction which she offered to use on the arm to cool it. I could see no harm in it and she assured me it had saved the leg of one of the farm hands the previous year, by cooling a fever. I asked if she had paper and ink as I wanted to get a message to Dr Darwin or at least to the Cheque Clerk at Haywood Junction. This proved a more difficult matter.

I was eventually able to write a note and send it by one of the farm hands to the Cheque Clerk with a request that he send it on with a rider to the Doctor at Derby. As he had seen the warrant I felt sure he would do this. Then, as Scipio was sleeping quietly again now, I pulled on my coat and went in search of the kind Methodist farmer who had taken us in, for I wanted to thank him. I also wanted to ascertain the exact circumstances in which he had found Scipio.

I found myself in a well-kept farmyard with barns and sheds that went down almost to the edge of the outside bank of the canal itself. The day was still, frosty and clear with a bright, low sun. From the dairy came the clitter-clatter and chatter of girls at work and from a barn beyond came the cheerful sound of someone whistling. Scattered fowls pecked at the frost-hardened ground under the watchful eye of a cockerel who surveyed them from the top of a frozen heap of manure. The scene, so peaceful and yet so industrious, so calm and yet so busy, seemed such a strange contrast to the last few days of fruitless stress and tension that I felt as if I had strayed into some completely foreign land.

My reverie was interrupted by the very person I had come to look for. The whistling ceased and the farmer himself appeared, stomping out of the barn. "Gud arternoon, Doctor," he said when he saw me. "And haa's tha patient fairin'?"

"The surgeon has been and set the broken bone," I said, "but Dr Trim is the doctor in charge, not me. You see, I'm not really ..."

"Ah, Dr Trim!" said the farmer enthusiastically. "Reet top doctor is Dr Trim."

"I can't thank you enough for all your kindness," I said. "I have sent off a letter today to my master, Dr Darwin of Derby. I hope we might be able to move Mr Africanus in the Doctor's carriage as soon as the surgeon says he is fit to travel. I am afraid all this is putting you to a great deal of trouble!"

"'Tis nowt," said the farmer kindly. "Tha munna make 'im to flit from 'ere 'til he be better. Poar fellow, us thought he were dead when us did find 'im. On t'road to t'class meeting ah was – and t'lass. She'd just stopped ba t'cottage yonder to call for one on t'class and there he be, lying in t'long grass and wet through wi' them terrible things on 'is wrists!"

"What time was it then?" I asked.

"Oh nigh noon," he replied, confirming what his daughter had told me. "Haa'd 'e come there, Doctor? – and when? Tha wast looking for 'im, tha sest."

I did some rapid calculations. If the *Robert* had arrived at Haywood junction at ten twenty, Scipio could well have been lying on the bank soaking wet, having presumably struggled out of the canal where he had been dumped and into the weeds at the bank, for as much as three hours. Once again I blamed myself for not have kept a better look out after the incidents with the *Robin* and at Colwich Lock. Out loud I said, "He was stolen by a former master who wanted to take him back to the West Indies where he would sell him."

"Well then, haa cum 'e be here? That's what ah doan't fathom."

I explained about the waybill, although I did not mention the treasure, and he was enthusiastic. "To think o' doin' that! Now tha cum in t'kitchen and tell t'hands that tale – jain us for a bite o' snap!"

With the farm hands in the kitchen for the midday meal I gladly recounted Scipio's adventure. You should have seen their faces when I told them that a manacled man had been thrown into the freezing canal! I could tell it would not have gone well with the Herrod brothers if these solid looking lads had caught up with them. To the rest of the conversation, which seemed to veer between preparing the ground to sow oats and some obscure boundary dispute with a neighbouring farm, I did not have much to contribute. However, the bread and cheese was certainly welcome and I was just finishing the very last crumb when the Ellen appeared again, her pretty face creased with worry.

"Can you come up, please, Doctor?" she asked, "I fear he's worse."

I followed her up to the little bedroom with a sense of foreboding. Scipio was strong but he had been through a lot. Had the bone-setting proved too much for him after all?

Scipio was indeed much worse. His eyes had a wild look and he was muttering to himself. I felt his brow: it was feverish. I felt his arm: it was not hot.

"Have you been applying lotions to that arm?" I asked Ellen.

"Yes, Sir," she replied with a worried look. "Have I done wrong, Sir?"

I shook my head. "His arm is cool but he seems feverish. I think he has caught a chill after being so cold and wet for so long."

The girl brightened up at once. "Oh, Sir, I have just the thing for that – elderberry. I have some left of my own bottling." And she hurried off to prepare her concoction.

It could do no harm, I thought, though looking at Scipio I wondered how it could be got into him. I bent over him and laid my hand on his forehead again.

"Matt!" he cried. "Oh Matt, I'm so glad you've come. I need to tell you where it is. I've been looking for you all over the place but it is so cold ..."

"Lie still old fellow," I soothed. "Don't worry about a thing. Just rest now."

"But I must go and find it!"

"You are not quite well enough to go looking for anything yet," I said gently. "Just lie still and rest. Plenty of time to go finding things when you are better."

"No, no, we must go now!" His voice had a note of panic, fevered and insistent. "How long have I been here? It may be too late already!"

"Just rest, Scipio," I said gently. "Don't worry. Everything is being taken care of. Dr Darwin is on his way."

Scipio passed his hand across his eyes. Then he spoke again, slowly, as though making a great effort. "The money. Your money ..."

I had been so concerned about my friend that the stolen money had almost disappeared from my mind but it had obviously been worrying Scipio – perhaps to the extent of making him feverish in his weakened state. I hastened to reassure him. "Don't worry; Will has it in hand. Whatever happens, the *Robert* will be stopped at Mr Wedgwood's wharf at Etruria. Will has a warrant; he's gone on ahead. He went to the local magistrate for help last night. They'll search the *Robert* if they find it on the canal. Now, you must rest or I am in danger of losing something far more valuable than the money!"

But Scipio did not sink back on his pillows with a sigh and close his eyes as I had hoped. Instead he raised himself up on his good arm and spoke as though making a superhuman effort. "Matt! The money is not on the boat. They have taken it away. It is hidden."

Chapter thirteen

THE TUNNEL

1794

Before, with shuddering limbs cold Tremor reels,
And Fever's burning nostril dogs his heels;
Loud claps the grinning Fiend his iron hands,
Stamps with his marble feet, and shouts along the lands;
Withers the damask cheek, unnerves the strong,
And drives with scorpion-lash the shrieking throng.

(Erasmus Darwin: The Botanic Garden. Part II.)

t Scipio's words I confess I was thrown into confusion. For a moment my heart sank. If I had thought about the money at all since finding Scipio, I had considered its recovery as some kind of forgone conclusion to be safely accomplished by Will and Mr Wedgwood. Did Scipio have information that contradicted my assumptions or was he raving because of the fever? Then my new professionalism reasserted itself. If Scipio was my patient – let alone my friend – I must put his welfare before any personal considerations. Whatever happened he must not be allowed to become overexcited.

"You must just rest now, Scipio," I said gently. "Don't worry about anything. Try to sleep and it will help you to get well."

He stared at me with wild eyes as though horrified that I was ignoring his words. Again he spoke, and, though perfectly coherent, he sounded as though the effort he was making to speak in a rational tone was almost superhuman. "Matt! – you think I am raving. I am not. Please listen. The money is hidden. It is not on the boat. I can tell you where it is."

He was becoming agitated now. I put my hand on his brow again. He was more feverish. I could see that he would only become worse if I continued to try to divert his attention from what he was trying to tell me. Perhaps if I abandoned that tactic he would unburden himself and then become calm, allowing the fever to subside. It was a risk, of course, for if his words were just the product of a fevered brain, nothing I said would help and letting him speak would only make the situation worse. What should I do?

"Matt," again that urgent appeal.

"What is it old fellow? Take your time. I'm listening."

"There is no time ... the money. It is not on the boat. They hid it. The mouth of the tunnel. The iron posts ..."

I had noticed the posts at various points on the towpath and I knew what they were: strapping posts. Wherever a boat might have to stop, by a lock or at the mouth of a tunnel, there were the posts.

They were gnarled and scoured by the ropes used by the boatmen to slow their boats – which they did by the simple expedient of wrapping a length of rope round the post.

"There are two posts. A new one and and old one. The old one is loose. It will just pull out of the ground. The treasure is below it. I heard them. They will come back for it. As soon as they have passed Etruria ..."

I looked at his wildly staring eyes. "Scipio, I understand. Don't worry. We'll get a search organised. But you must promise to rest quietly or I certainly cannot leave you to go in search of treasure!"

He lay back on the pillows at once. "Yes ..." he said and already the tone was less firm and forceful. "Yes ... I can lie here ..."

The door opened and Ellen reappeared carrying a delicate teacup in which some brew or other was steaming. "How is he, doctor?" she asked quietly. "Can he take this, do you think, if we spoon it in?" And she sat down on the chair beside the bed.

"Go, Matt," said Scipio. "You must go and look now before they come back."

"I'll go," I said, "but if I do you must lie very quiet and drink what the kind young lady here has brought you."

As I spoke there was the sound of wheels in the yard below. I looked out of the window and to my great joy and astonishment beheld Doctor Darwin's carriage pulling in through the gate.

"Scipio," I said, "Dr Darwin has just come. I will tell him what you told me at once. He will know what to do. But you must take your medicine and lie here in complete quiet."

He fell back on the pillows exhausted and his voice sank to a whisper. "Praise the Lord!" he said.

At first I was astounded that the Doctor had arrived so soon. Surely he had not had my message yet!

"I was in this d-direction m-making a c-call on a p-patient," he explained, "and I t-took the opportunity to c-call at the office at the j-junction in case there was n-news of you. I was there when your m-messenger c-came in."

"Can you come and have a look at him, Doctor?" I asked. "He was doing so well, but now he seems a little feverish."

The doctor looked doubtful. "He is Doctor Trim's p-patient," he said, "I can by all m-means go up and have a l-look – but not in a p-professional capacity."

"I quite understand," I said, adding with a touch of pride, "although they keep insisting that *I* am the doctor..."

"Is there any n-news of W-Will?" asked Dr Darwin. "I g-gathered from the cheque c-clerk that he went charging off to Etruria at f-first l-light this m-morning – Mr Anson would not let a p-party set out overnight – to intercept the *R-Robert.*"

I had a mental picture of Will boiling with frustration at being held back by a magistrate. Mr Anson must be a forceful, as well as a sensible person, I thought! "I'm not sure what they will find if they do catch her," I said, "Scipio has just come out with a strange story – although it may just be the result of a fevered imagination, of course," and I told him what Scipio had said about the treasure and the strapping post.

The Doctor listened gravely. "That sounds a l-little t-too exact and reasonable for a f-fevered b-brain," he said, "and I think it should b-be investigated." He looked at his pocket watch. "I have one more c-call to m-make and it is urgent. I'll g-go and have a l-look at Scipio. Then give m-me an hour to m-make my c-call and get b-back here and I'll t-take you to the t-tunnel m-mouth in my c-carriage. We'll see what there is to be f-found." The narrow stairs creaked and groaned under his weight as he ascended and I followed him.

Scipio, lying calmly on his pillow, his broken arm propped up exactly in accordance with the surgeon's instructions, looked the model patient. Ellen, empty teacup in hand, made a graceful curtsy to the Doctor and then politely left the little room.

"Is he still f-feverish?" asked the Doctor. "If you are in charge here, M-Matthew you had better f-find out."

I put my hand on Scipio's brow. The fever had definitely lessened almost to nothing. I checked the broken arm. Still cool. I felt rather foolish to have been so alarmed – or perhaps hot elderberry cordial was really the elixir the farm girl had claimed!

"Scipio," said the Doctor, "I understand you have g-given Matthew s-some very valuable information. R-rest assured, it will be acted on as p-promptly as p-possible."

"Thank you, Sir," said Scipio very quietly.

"We c-can arrange for s-someone to look after you here until you are w-well enough to c-come home." He turned to me. "B-best f-find that young w-woman or s-someone again," he said, "she looked c-competent enough. He's clearly n-not feverish, and is m-making a g-good recovery," and, closing the door behind us so quietly it was almost dainty, he made his ponderous way down the stairs.

The Doctor set off again in his carriage, promising to return as soon as he could and old Annie was sent for to continue the watch over the patient. I dared not watch myself for fear Scipio would become agitated that I was still at his bedside and not seeking out the treasure at the mouth of the tunnel.

At first I sat quietly in the little farm parlour reading the copy of *Rights of Man* that had been in my pocket, thinking that it would distract me from the anxious thoughts which would keep arising despite my confidence in the Doctor. I thumbed back and forth for a while trying to reconcile Paine's idea of a constitution with his ideas of law. He seemed to argue that no one can make binding laws for future generations; there has to be a right to change things. After that he seemed also to be saying that a country's constitution is binding on future generations and that the people of a country must make its constitution. This seemed arbitrary. Why could a constitution, once made, be unchangeable by future generations and yet laws must be subject to change?

The minutes grew into hours and the Doctor did not reappear. I gave up trying to sort out inconsistencies in what I was reading. Where was he? If he did not hurry up we would be reduced to trying to look in the dark! I was just becoming desperate when there was a clatter of hooves in the yard and a lone horseman appeared. I was trying to master my disappointment that it was not the Doctor's carriage that had arrived when a thunderous knocking on the farmhouse door was followed by the entrance of Will, looking as if he had been riding with the furies behind him.

"Thank goodness I've found you," he panted. "The Cheque Clerk told me where to go. I gather you've found Scipio. Has Dr Darwin been here? Wedgwood had the boat searched. They found nothing! Had to let them go! I followed her to Longport – they've abandoned her. I went over her from stem to stern and I could not find a thing ..."

"Will! Will!" I said holding up my hand. "I've found out where it is! It's hidden in the mouth of that tunnel. There is a loose strapping post. All we have to do is get there before they return for it. I'm just waiting for Dr Darwin to come back."

"You're waiting!" he exploded. "Haven't they got any horses we can borrow here? It's what – four miles back to the tunnel from here? It must be near that place where we had that trouble with the *Robin*. We can get there in no time ... If Dr Darwin wants to come afterwards ..."

He swept me off to find some horses. Farmer Samuel was willing to help. Will was cagey about exactly what we were looking for but the farmer promised to explain where we had gone to Dr Darwin when he returned. In what felt like no time at all we were dashing off along the rutted road in a thin cold drizzle back towards the tunnel mouth.

It was beginning to get dark. It was very cold indeed by the time we reached the point where the road crossed the tunnel but Will's enthusiasm for immediate action was not at all abated.

"We can leave the horses here under these trees for a bit of shelter while we go down and find the stuff," he said, making it sound simple. "I hope we are in time."

I hoped so too but somehow that awful moment when we reopened the desk and found the treasure was not there kept returning to my mind. Snatches of sermons on the providence of God (a favourite topic with Mr Archer) kept coming back to me too, snatches that dealt with the unpleasant way things may turn out and yet still be for our ultimate good. Was I just not meant to have that money?

We made our way cautiously along the path down the steep bank towards the tunnel mouth. As it came into view we stopped abruptly. A lantern was glowing feebly inside the tunnel and by its light we could just make out a moving figure.

"That's torn it!" I whispered in horror through chattering teeth. "What on earth can we do now?"

Will had had a tough upbringing. He had only survived by standing up for himself. Our previous hostile encounter with canal boatmen had unnerved me but Will was undaunted. He was also a born strategist. "Only one thing to do," he murmured. "If he's on his own we'll bring it off. We'll get down to those bushes right by the mouth of the tunnel and then we'll spring on him. You get his eyes covered; I'll do the rest. C'mon." And, before I had time to think about it, he was off slinking down towards the bushes.

In absolute terror I followed Will. At the very brink of the canal he stopped. Putting his mouth to my ear he whispered, "When I say 'now,' we rush him. Get your hands over his eyes from behind and hang on. Leave the rest to me."

I could see the figure more clearly now. The old strapping post lay on the ground beside him and he was squatting on his heels on the towpath holding up the lantern with one hand and reaching deep into the hole where the post had been with the other. As we crept up behind him he gave a kind of grunt of satisfaction and stood up, still with his back to us. "Now!" whispered Will.

I don't know to this day how I summoned up the nerve but at Will's word of command I leapt at the back of the figure and flung my hands round his face. At the same time Will grabbed his legs and we all fell onto the towpath. The lantern clattered over and went out. There was a dull thud as some heavy thing hit the path and then in the gloom I could suddenly distinguish the man's legs kicking out frantically, not at us but at the large canvas bag that had fallen as Will tackled him. "Watch out!" I cried. "He'll have it in the canal!"

But it was too late. There was a splash: into the water it went and sank like a stone. And now the man was really struggling. Will had got on top of him and I hung on but it was clearly only a matter of time before he got away. He was a small fellow but wiry and even Will had a job to keep a grip on him. "Don't let him go, the villain!" Will was shouting when suddenly a shape loomed up from inside the tunnel and then stopped politely in front of us. It was a horse.

"You in trouble, Sirs?" came a voice from within the darkness of the tunnel and a boat, gliding along behind the now stationary animal, seemed to grow up round it.

"Yes!" shouted Will urgently. "Rope! Rope. I must have rope or this thief will get away!"

Herrod, for it was indeed he, trussed like a fowl ready for the spit and swearing and cursing, was heaved aboard the narrow-boat. The astonished steersman and his companion had provided a quantity of rope enough to tie up a whole gang of robbers from their store of worn tow ropes and Will had made an expert job of tying and gagging our captive.

"What's happened, masters?" The steersman asked anxiously. "Is he a highwayman? There was one of his type come down on the canal to escape justice last year, so I heard."

Will got out his warrant. "He's a common robber," he explained, "and I have a warrant for his arrest.

The magistrate is on the look out for him at Haywood Junction."

"Mr Anson?" said the steersman. "We're going through the junction and then on to Stourport. If Mr Anson will vouch for you I can take you on there."

Will looked at me. "I'd be very grateful, thank you," he said simply. "But we have horses up on the road above the tunnel so my friend here, Mr Batchelor, will have to stay to look after them. Also," he hesitated, "also something has fallen into the canal You don't have an old spare boat hook or anything we could borrow, do you?"

The steersman laughed. "Lost his ill-gotten gains in the canal, has he?" he said.

Chapter fourteen

LOST AND FOUND

1794

Or where cold dews their secret channels lave,
And Earth's dark chambers hide the stagnant wave,
O, pierce, YE NYMPHS! her marble veins, and lead
Her gushing fountains to the thirsty mead;
Wide o'er the shining vales, and trickling hills
Spread the bright treasure in a thousand rills.

(Erasmus Darwin, The Botanic Garden. Part I)

I was cold. My teeth were chattering and now my whole frame seemed to be shivering in reaction to all the excitement. Whatever happened I must not go back without finding the treasure now! The upset lantern was still lying on the towpath so I set it to rights and lit it again with my own tinder and flint. Then I grasped the borrowed boathook and poked it into the water.

It was not easy to remember where exactly the canvas bag of treasure had fallen. I turned to face the canal just at the point opposite the remaining strapping post and began fishing about in earnest.

How far out had the bag fallen? How deep was the water further out? I peered into the murk. I had no answer to either of these questions but it was getting darker rapidly so I decided to work as systematically as I could.

I wielded that boathook until my arms were utterly stiff with cold. The most exciting thing I caught was a short length of old tow rope. Where was the bag? I was so chilled now that my fingers could hardly grasp the hook. I was almost in despair when I noticed that the very length of the tool I was using was making me tend to leave out the most likely area of search. I began again, working my way methodically along the area I had selected but this time keeping right up to the very edge of the canal, holding the boathook vertical. Within moments the hook struck something hard and lumpy and I knelt down and peered excitedly at the water in the light of the lantern. The canal edge seemed shallow so I abandoned the hook, plunging my hands and arms into the freezing water. I felt anxiously about. It would never do to grasp the bag at the wrong end and scatter the precious contents all over the bottom of the canal. Ah! Here was the drawstring – and yes! – the mouth of the bag itself, still pulled safely shut. But now my numbed fingers were becoming so stiff with cold I could not force them to get a grip on it. At last I somehow managed to slide enough of my agonised hand into the loop of the drawstring and drag the bag to the surface by raising my arm. I was in the very act of hauling my precious find out of the water when there was a raucous shout from above the tunnel mouth behind me:

"M-Matthew!"

For just a moment I was so terrified, my nerves already worked up to such a pitch, that I almost dropped my treasure back into the canal. Then relief flooded over me. "I'm here, Doctor!" I cried, "and I've found it!"

I remember little of the journey back to Derby in the Doctor's carriage. Back at Full Street, I can only just recall him solemnly sealing the bag and giving me a receipt for it before stowing it away in the great iron strong box in his study. Then Mrs B was putting a hot drink of something into my hand and pushing me towards the attic stairs. "Go on up with you to bed! I never heard the like! Charging up and down the navigation at this time of night! And in the depth of winter too. You'll catch your death, you will, you foolish lad. And you thinking you'll train to be a real doctor! And there's a warming pan put in your bed so mind you take it out!"

I did remember the pan. Then I crept into the comfort of a warm bed. A blackness fell over me that was so deep and dreamless that Number Three Full Street could have been reduced to rubble around me by an earthquake without waking me.

When I did wake it was still dark. The sky was clear and moonless and the familiar stars shone through my tiny uncurtained window. I was warm. I listened. The house was silent. No stirring of the kitchen maid in the attic room opposite mine. No clatter of an early cart in the street. As if to satisfy my vague curiosity about the time, All Saints' Church clock struck a majestic four. I was warm. Why was that so particularly good? I had been cold earlier ... very cold ... Everything came flooding back into my mind like the rush of water into a lock when you raise the paddle. Scipio! My treasure! Every problem I had ever had was solved. Everything was going to be fine. Scipio was getting better, I could go to Edinburgh and train as a proper doctor. All my worries were at an end. I could turn over and go back to sleep knowing that tomorrow I would begin a new life, a life I had never dared to dream of. And yet ... Why was there still that sense of unease? Something not right, outstanding, not dealt with, a clash of outlooks seemed hanging over me demanding that I deal with it.

A familiar jumble of words rose in my mind. "If we know the Saviour ... we can know Him personally ... Come and welcome ..." that was Mr Archer's voice. "Resting in Jesus ... It is all joy to know Him ... nothing can harm us, His children ..." that was Scipio's deep well-modulated voice.

Then came another voice, "B-beneath the s-sea ... a f-filament ... the f-first c-cause ... you c-can c-call it God for c-convenience if you wish ..."

The clash of voices resolved itself. Suddenly I was wide awake. Wider awake than I had ever been in my life. I understood what it was. If the Doctor was right, if the universe was the result of a first cause which could be *called* God for convenience, how *could* we know him personally? That concept had no meaning. But if Mr Archer was right, if Scipio was right, if it was true, if it was possible to know God and I passed by the opportunity to have this knowledge, no matter how much money I now had or did not have, I would build my life on a falsehood. And not only my *life* ... It was vital. I had to know the truth! But how? What did it matter whether I was well off or poor?

Surely to know God, to know His Son, to have everlasting life in a glorious heaven with Him in the end left everything else I had struggled to regain just an empty, dripping canvas bag.

Scipio's voice came to me again from the jumbled memory of the last few days, "You must seek Him and seek Him now ... Pray, Matt! Pray."

I got out of the pleasant warmth of my bed and knelt on the bare, cold, wooden floor. How often had I heard Mr Archer pray? How many prayer meetings had I attended? I realised with horror that I had never, ever prayed myself at all. "I can't do it for you," Scipio's words again. I groaned. And then in absolute despair I cried out, "Lord Jesus Christ, I cannot pray. But I know that You can. Pray for me and I know that God will hear the prayer I cannot say. How can I live my life without

You to guide me? How can I die without You to save me? I do not want to spend eternity in that terrible place of punishment You have reserved for sinners!" My teeth were chattering now but I could not stop. "Could I have that grace of trusting Your Word? Could I not be Your servant too? That would be more precious than any gold."

At that point Edward, whose little room was next to mine and separated by only the thinnest of partitions, banged on the wall.

"Oi, Matthew, quieten down, there's a good fellow! I have to get up in the morning to see to the Doctor's horse!"

Trembling, I crept back into bed. What did it matter if I went to Edinburgh or not? I had thought finding my treasure was the most important thing in my whole life. Now I knew that it was not. This was more important. Would my prayer be answered? "Hear my prayer, Lord," I whispered as I shivered under the blankets. "I understand now how worthless anything else is."

I woke the next morning to the sound of All Saints' bells going full pelt. I was staggered that I had slept for so long. I struggled into my clothes as quickly as I could for fear there would be nothing in the kitchen for me to eat if I did not get there before Mrs B left for church. Thank goodness the chapel service was not until eleven. I clattered down the stairs before the bells changed to their single warning note but alas, Mrs B had already gone. Unabashed, I helped myself from the bread crock and the butter dish. I rinsed my plate in the scullery where, thanks to the Doctor's ingenuity, the clean water from the hills welled up in a never ending supply, flowed through a trough and out by a pipe into the Derwent. And all the time it was hammering in my head, "more precious than gold, more precious than gold ..."

I took myself off to the chapel, slipped in and sat down at the back in a corner. I bowed my head to pray and the words were still there, "more precious than gold, more precious ..." When Mr Archer stood up in the pulpit he looked tired, as though he too had wakened in the night to wrestle with things he did not understand. He preached, or rather tried to preach, on a passage from Romans but it was not his best effort and I could see that other members of the congregation were fidgeting. I tried hard to concentrate.

"None of the fallen race of man can entertain a rational hope of glory, but what must be founded on Christ alone ..." What was a rational hope of glory? Perhaps my hope was irrational? But I did understand, now, that Christ was more precious, that He was what I wanted above all things.

"Have you then any hope of eternal happiness? A hope founded on Christ alone? Have you seen yourself hopeless and undone without Him, a hell-bound sinner?"

"Yes," I thought miserably, "I have."

"Have you been brought to give up any hope that is based on the littleness of your sins or the sufficiency of your good deeds to counterbalance them?"

"Yes," I thought, again miserably. "I understand all that." I remembered Doctor Darwin's idea of sympathy balancing the misery of the world to give equilibrium and realised with a shock that the idea of a balance between good and evil was ridiculous. How could heaven be heaven if it was full of half-bad people? No, that would not be heaven! Heaven would be the glory of truly knowing Christ and being totally and absolutely without *any* trace of evil or sin.

Mr Archer was now adopting his most lecturing and hectoring style, a very tone of voice that usually made my mind wander to more interesting subjects. But today, despite *how* he said it, my mind was riveted by *what* he was saying. To my astonishment he seemed to describe exactly what I was thinking. "If you have so often heard heaven described by ministers and Christians, that you cannot help admitting that it is the presence of God and the Lamb that makes up the blessedness of saints in glory; let me ask, does this *really* seem to you a glorious idea? Is it a view of heaven that suits your taste? If God would offer to make a heaven for you, just how you wanted it, what would your idea of it be? Would nothing satisfy you but to behold His face in righteousness, and to be fully conformed to His likeness?"

Suddenly something seemed to click in my head like one of the Doctor's microscope slides coming into focus. I *did* feel like that. Most earnestly I did. I almost jumped up to shout, "Yes!" I was so deeply surprised at myself. I longed to know Christ more than anything.

"If you can honestly say, 'Whom have I in heaven but Thee,' you will also be able to add, 'and there is none upon earth that I desire besides Thee.'" His voice droned on urging his concern for those who did *not* long to know the Saviour and who were trusting in their own goodness but to me it was suddenly clear.

To truly long to know Him above all else, to know your own worthlessness and your need of Him, *is* to know Him – for how else could we come? – and to be on the path to knowing Him truly for ever.

At the end of the service I stood up dazed. We had sung but I could not have told you what. There were tears streaming down my face and I bent my head to hide them while I groped for my handkerchief.

A hand gripped my arm and I looked up.

"Will!" I was surprised. His face looked haggard, his jacket was torn and his breeches spattered with mud. I would not normally have expected to see him in chapel in such a state but his appearance barely registered with me now. I was so bursting with the good news I wanted to tell him and I was sure he would want to hear.

"Matt! Did you find it? Have you got it safe? Did you find your treasure?" Will's voice was tired but insistent.

"Yes!" I replied. "Oh Will! I have found a priceless treasure. I have found something more precious than gold!"

Will looked strangely embarrassed. Perhaps it was the sight of my tear-stained face. He twisted his hat round and round in his hands. "Well, hmm ... that's good. I'm glad to hear it. But, er, I take it you found the money as well?"

Before I could do more than nod, a gentle tug on my sleeve distracted me. I looked round to find Susan from the farm looking anxiously at me.

"Mr Africanus," she began, "Is he safe?"

"Yes, he's safe," I replied. "He was suffering from cold and has broken his arm but he is being well cared for."

"Oh where is he?" she cried, sounding quite distressed.

"He is at a farm by the canal and quite safe," I assured her again.

"Where is it? Do you think they would let me come and nurse him? I'd be no trouble ..."

"Well, it's a long way from here, Colwich Farm near Haywood – but ..."

"Colwich Farm! By the navigation? Oh! That's where my mother's old sister, Aunt Annie, is in service. What a providential thing! I'm sure I could go there if ..."

"Oh, you don't need to worry," I smiled, "he's being very well looked after by the farmer's young daughter, a clever and competent lass." As soon as the words were out of my mouth I realised it was the wrong thing to have said.

"Oh is she!" she said wildly. "I must go ... How ..."

"Steady on," said Will, and he sat down on the pew bench like a man who can no longer stand up. "Look, don't you go fretting to traipse over half the county just yet. Give Mr Matthew here and me a couple of days and if we haven't got something sorted out for you by then, well, we'll see to it that you can get there." This would have sounded more convincing if it had not been followed by a huge yawn.

As editor of the *Derby Mercury* Will had immense prestige but even so Susan was not to be put off.

"What sort of thing, Mr Ward, Sir?" she asked, "and how would you see to it?"

Will waved his hands. "Can't tell you – newspaper policy – but don't you worry, take my word for it."

And with that she had to be content.

"Look, Matt," said Will, as Susan drifted off, "I've ridden all night to get here. Tell me, have you got it safe?"

I nodded again.

"Good," he said and he sounded immensely relieved. "In that case I'm off to my room at the *Mercury* office for a sleep for I'm too tired to speak. Come round before the evening service and I'll tell you all about it."

Chapter fifteen

LASTING TREASURE

1794

So when with light and shade, concordant strife!
Stern CLOTHO weaves the chequer'd thread of life;
Hour after hour the growing line extends,
The cradle and the coffin bound its ends ...

(Erasmus Darwin, The Botanic Garden. Part II.)

After chapel the Doctor sent for me.

"Ah, M-Matthew," he said as I entered the study, "you look b-better for some s-sleep. I heartily c-congratulate you on recovering your f-fortune and t-tomorrow, if you wish, I c-can help you d-decide the best way to d-dispose of it s-so as to give you a s-sufficient income to allow you t-to s-study m-medicine at Edinburgh. I p-presume that is what you would wish t-to d-do?"

"Indeed, Sir," I said, "unless you would suggest anywhere else?"

"N-no, I think Edinburgh is the b-best place for a young m-man such as yourself to g-go for m-medical study, so long as you k-keep an open m-mind."

"An open mind, Sir?"

"An open m-mind, M-Matthew. T-test and evaluate everything c-carefully and d-do not accept as an unalterable t-truth anything which you have not s-seen s-sufficiently p-proved. When I was at Edinburgh m-myself the t-teaching was – well a little too m-mechanistic in its understanding of bodily f-functions, shall we s-say. You certainly have the d-diligence to make real h-headway in m-medicine. Keep an open m-mind, do your own research and if you c-come b-back to this part of the world to p-practice after you have qualified, I can see us welcoming you to the L-Lunar S-Society."

"Thank you, Sir," I said carefully for although I would once have regarded this as the fulfilment of a dream, I realised, almost with surprise, that it was an honour I no longer yearned to receive. My hand stole involuntarily to the little gold trinket that was still in my pocket.

The doctor smiled. "You d-do not s-seem to relish the p-prospect, Matthew," he said shrewdly.

"Indeed, Sir ..." I began but he continued.

"We have p-prominent d-dissenters as well as at least one c-clergyman and a Quaker among our n-number in the Lunar S-Society. You have n-no need to fear that your c-connection with W-William W-Ward and his b-baptist f-friends would hinder you. All religious p-persuasions are welcome am-m-mong us."

I wondered however I could explain to him what I had experienced, but explain it I must, so I began in a rush, "You have been very kind to me, Sir, but I must tell you that I have made a discovery which has changed my life. You say that I should be careful not accept as unalterable truth anything which is not sufficiently proved. I agree that this is an excellent principle. In order to carry it out in some areas such as morality or philosophy or theology there must be some absolute standard against which to measure the proposition in question. In such areas one idea measured against an other idea can give no inkling of the truth of either." I paused for breath, quite astounded at what I had managed to say.

"G-go on," he urged quietly.

I took a deep breath wondering if I could, in fact, go on and found myself saying, "I have discovered this standard, indeed looking back, I find I have known it for a long time: it is the Word of God. In measuring my life and principles against that standard I found myself totally wanting. But not until last night did I fully understand that there is someone whose life meets this standard who was prepared to lay it down, to sacrifice it, for me. He is not just some Great First Cause; He is a person. He is the person who not only created the universe but told us how and when He did it in the book He has written."

"And l-last n-night?" His tone was curious and a strange smile played on his lips.

"Last night I put my faith and trust in Jesus Christ as my Saviour and as a result I began seriously comparing some of the ideas you have taught me about the origins of life, for instance, against that standard. I find they do not measure up to it. I am, and ever will be, grateful to you, Sir, for your kindness to me and your help to me when I had, or thought I had, not a penny to my name. I ask you to forgive me and not think me ungrateful or churlish after all you have done for me. I have no right to comment as a mere ignorant doctor's assistant on the ideas of the great philosophical minds of the Lunar Society but, God helping me, I intend to live my life in His service and in the light of His Word for I am fully convinced that it is true in every particular from beginning to end."

"M-Matthew, Matthew," he said gently shaking his massive head, "the t-tide is not running in your f-favour. The time is c-coming when all but the most ignorant p-peasant will admit the t-truth. The B-Bible has some good things in it, no doubt, but as a t-textbook of history only the n-naïve will openly c-claim it to b-be accurate." He paused for a moment then sighed and said gently, "Matthew, Ad-d-dam and Eve are just the n-names of two Egyptian hieroglyphic f-figures representing the early state of m-mankind; Abel was the n-name of an hieroglyphic f-figure representing the age of p-p-pasturage, and Cain the n-name of another hieroglyphic symbol representing the age of agriculture, at which t-time the uses of iron were d-discovered. As the p-people who cultivated the earth and b-built houses would increase in n-numbers much f-faster by their greater p-production of f-food, they would readily conquer or d-destroy the p-people who were s-sustained by p-pasturage – which was t-typified by C-Cain slaying Abel. Do you n-not s-see? It is n-not at all as you think. I could g-go on ... Such things are n-not said openly by the wise at the m-moment but they are b-becoming – and will b-become – obvious. In the Church and in D-Dissent the most far-s-sighted, the most energetic wonder about these things p-privately and will d-discuss them – when and where it is s-safe to d-do s-so."

"Sir, you say the tide is running against me. It may be so," I answered, "but it will turn. I believe you are wrong and therefore however long it takes, truth will out, as the saying is." Then I added hastily, "I hope you do not think me rude," for in the effort of thinking out what to say I had quite forgotten my manners.

"P-power is on your s-side, M-matthew, now." he said with a smile and waving aside my apology, "b-but the day is c-coming, though I may n-not live to see it, when if you do n-not change your op-p-pinions it will be M-Matthew B-Batchelor *contra mundum.*"

I did not like to admit that I didn't know what he was talking about.

165

My encounter with the Doctor left me feeling almost dazed. I did not know where in my mind I had dredged up my remarks from. I hurried eagerly over to Market Head as soon as it could decently be considered to be "before the evening service" to see what Will thought. Something was puzzling me in his behaviour too. Why had his reaction to my joyful news this morning been so uncomfortable? Was it just that he was tired out with having ridden all night from somewhere beyond Etruria? Or could it be that perhaps even Will ...?

Will himself opened the side door of the *Mercury* Office to me. He looked much refreshed, though his hair was rumpled and he was blinking like someone who has just woken up.

"Matt!" he exclaimed, "Sorry I put you off earlier! I was feeling worn out, I can tell you, with that ride and then what with Susan going on ..."

"That's understandable, Will," I said, relieved, "although I don't know quite what you are going to do to help her."

"Not *absolutely* sure myself, yet," he admitted, "but Scipio is getting better at a phenomenal rate and I'm sure Mr Drury will want him back here as soon as possible."

"I was beginning to think you were not particularly pleased with my good news!" I said as he beckoned me in to the newspaper office.

"Not pleased?" he laughed. "I'm completely delighted! It is wonderful news! We outwitted those thieves and cleared Scipio's name – not to mention regaining your fortune. I looked in on Scipio at the farm before I left and I gather he has quite a tale to tell. Mr Anson's been wonderful. Herrod's been charged and is under lock and key and his brother was rounded up just beyond Longport. The magistrates will take a pretty dim view of it all and Renshaws are prosecuting for damage to the *Robert* and loss of goods. Not that that's to be compared to kidnapping and attempted murder. They'll be lucky not to hang even though Scipio is an ex-slave."

"Oh!" I said feeling crestfallen. "That's not what I meant. I've found a better treasure, Will. All this time I've been longing to know the Saviour and thinking it was somehow impossible but I've found Him, Will."

He looked down at his boots and mumbled, "That's good news too, of course." It sounded so lame that I knew at once that I had something now that Will did not have – at least not yet.

I wondered what to say but before I could think of a way of proceeding he said quietly, "You know, Matt, I've been ruminating about Paine's ideas lately quite a lot – in between all the other things that have happened. I'm beginning to think that Scipio might be right."

I was glad he was reconsidering at least that aspect of his ideas. I began to lay out to him what I concluded about Paine's remarks on laws and constitutions. In fact, we settled down to a long discussion which was almost like old times. I say *almost* for I felt a strange tinge of sadness because I could find no way to communicate to him the cause of my newfound contentment.

It was later in the week that I saw Mr Archer and his joy and enthusiasm almost made up for Will's lack of it. He listened entranced while I went over the whole story. I did not tell him about Dr Darwin's philosophical beliefs as I considered they had been told me in strict confidence. I knew the Doctor considered it could ruin his practice if they became public knowledge. This was why he never put his name on his published poetry. I did, however, mention the Doctor's final remark. "What does it mean," I asked him, "Matthew Batchelor *contra mundum?* I have enough Latin to know the words mean 'against the world' but the Doctor said it as though they had some significance which I ought to recognise."

"They are reputed to be the words of Athanasius," he replied, "a great teacher of the middle ages who defended the doctrine of the Trinity and suffered much for his pains in an age which denied that teaching. *Athanasius contra mundum.* Perhaps the Doctor has leanings towards Unitarianism – like those espoused by the congregation at Friargate and so sees you in, as it were, an Athanasian light."

I did not tell him that the Doctor's beliefs went way beyond that. Thinking it over later, I felt that I was hardly worthy to be classed with such a person as Athanasius but I presumed the Doctor's words to be sarcastic. Nevertheless, as the days went on he was as kind to me as ever, helping me sort out my financial affairs and bank my assets and supporting my application to the University of Edinburgh with a personal letter.

At last all the jewellery was disposed of and a tidy sum banked at Newton's Bank under Mr Archer's watchful eye. I called on Mr Drury and tried to thank him formally for his kindness in insisting that the treasure was entirely mine. He would allow no hint that things could have been otherwise and was generous in his wishes for my success at Edinburgh – where he was certain, he said, I would be accepted.

Did I say all the jewellery? There was one small item I hung onto. It was that little golden trinket spangled with diamonds and shaped like a crescent moon. I was told by the jeweller that it had probably once formed part of a lady's old-fashioned ear-ring. Its value was modest compared to some of the other items but it was a pretty thing. It had been in my pocket all through my adventures and I did not sell it.

I was making my way down to the kitchen at Full Street one morning a few weeks later with a letter in my hand. The spring was late coming that year and the weather was still wintery. The Doctor, I assumed, was still out on his rounds; no doubt the slushy lanes slowed down even his wonderful carriage. It was Mrs Darwin therefore who stopped me as I came in from my work at the dispensary to give me the letter the post boy had just brought across from the inn. I knew that in a few minutes she would be sending for Mrs B to go over the coming week's meals and other house-keeping arrangements with her. The kitchen would be empty. I would be able to sit in comfort by the fire, read my letter undisturbed and solace myself with something edible should the news it contained prove disappointing. I had no letters as a rule and I knew this one must therefore relate to my application to study in Edinburgh.

As I approached the kitchen I was surprised to hear the sound of voices and laughter. I opened the door to find Mrs B, rolling pin in hand and seated with her by the table was Susan.

"Ah, Matt," said Mrs B beaming, "well, here's a piece of good news and no mistake."

I raised my eyebrows, "What good news is that, Mrs B?"

"Well now, best let them tell you themselves," she said mysteriously. "I dare say he'll be here in a minute. You sit by the fire and read your letter, Matt, and don't mind us."

I gave it up and did as I was instructed while Mrs B went on with a pastry-making demonstration to Susan who was drinking in a foolproof method for a specially light fruit tart. The letter was indeed from Edinburgh but so long and involved that it took me a while – especially against a background torrent of information about a "really good fire ... a moderate oven for light pastry: too quick will burn it, too slow will make it soddened" – to get to the relevant part. Just as I was beginning to work out that the intended message was indeed favourable there was a light tap on the kitchen door and in walked – Scipio.

I was so surprised I nearly dropped my precious letter in the fire!

"Scipio!" I almost yelled, "and looking as fit as a fiddle! How long have you been back in Derby?"

Indeed, he looked well. A light sling held his left arm but he was walking without the aid of any stick and smiling broadly.

"I returned only last night," he said and it was a joy to hear his rich cultured voice sounding clear and firm again. "Mr Drury advised me to come over to see Dr Darwin for advice about my arm, although it seems to me to be healing well – thanks in no small measure to your ministrations, Matt."

"Now tell Matt your news!" commanded Mrs B before I could make any kind of depreciating remark about my lack of medical skill. Susan's face coloured a sort of deep pink and she tried to look as if she was intent upon the now empty pastry board. Scipio, however, only smiled more broadly than ever.

"Miss Susan has done me the honour of consenting to become my wife," he explained with great dignity. "We are to be married, if the Lord wills, later in the spring."

Scipio's rich tones usually prompted me to a dignified response but before I could gather myself together with something suitable to the occasion, there was a screech from Mrs B about the forgotten tart now presumed reduced to cinders. For a few moments there was pandemonium in the kitchen while the tart – which looked delicious and highly edible to me when it emerged – was rescued.

When order was restored I said, "I offer you my heartiest congratulations," and then added, "and may God bless you both." I fumbled in my pocket. "May I have the pleasure of bestowing a small gift on the bride to be?" I put the glittering golden moon into the hand of the astonished Susan. It seemed a fitting thing to do. My desire to become a *Lunatick* had evaporated now and the little crescent had shrunk as a result. It was nothing more than a pretty trinket.

And now I must conclude my tale. Susan and Scipio settled down to a happy married life and were blessed with a large family. After my time in Edinburgh I was always welcome at their home – for I did return in the end to my native town. I even bought back that old desk of my grandmother's and had it moved to my own home. The Doctor had moved out of

Derby town and died not long afterwards but my new home was not far down Full Street near his old house. Here the desk's imposing bulk and massive solidity added a dignified air to my surgery.

I spent many happy evenings at the fireside of Scipio and Susan Africanus listening to Scipio's wise and beautifully enunciated words and romping with the ever-expanding brood of children. For the rest of his life Scipio never tired of telling how he spotted Herrod through the window on that day we found the treasure in the desk. He never tired also of telling the tale of the illiterate young boatman who so unselfishly ensured that his scrawled initials on the reverse of the waybill reached the newspaper office at Market Head in Derby. Of the fracas which had resulted in his broken arm he would never speak but I got the impression that getting Scipio into manacles must have taken almost superhuman effort.

Will did not remain in Derby. He went to Hull not long afterwards to another newspaper job and I lost touch with him for a while. Then one day a letter arrived at my lodgings in Edinburgh. He was going to India he said. "Matthew, I no longer fret about the rights of man," he wrote, "My concern is for the souls of men. I know Him! At last I understand what you were telling me. Rejoice with me, dear Matt!"

He went out to serve as a printer alongside a missionary, a Mr Carey, who had been sent to India by that very Northampton Association whose meeting had caused all the excitement at Agard Street on the day of Scipio's first appearance there. In this at least Dr Darwin had predicted correctly, William Ward was going to go far!

There is little more to tell of myself, and in any case I am bone weary of writing. I am Batchelor by name and bachelor by nature so I have no sons and daughters of my own to whom this tale could have been told, as it should have been, bit by bit. I have seen changes – reforms – in the electoral system that would have delighted Will if he had been here in England to enjoy them. And all without the horrors of a revolution like that of France, thanks in a great measure to preachers like old Mr Archer and his friends.

But Dr Erasmus Darwin's ideas rumble on and on and I have kept silent, thinking they would die away and the truth would triumph naturally. There was a moment of premature rejoicing about a year ago when I read of Louis Pasteur's experiments in France. That should put paid to any idea that life could somehow have arisen spontaneously, I thought. But no! Apparently it does not matter that it is now for ever proved that there is no way for the whole thing to even get started. That can just be ignored! And now this great overblown book has arrived, this *Origin of Species*. Here is my old master's grandson articulating the same folly! And he does it in such scientific sounding prose as will just tickle the ears of the present age – as his grandfather's pompous poetry did in his day.

And so the tide is coming in faster than ever: it has not yet turned. I will die before it does now. But turn it will one day; for truth does not depend on Matthew Batchelor – which is just as well. If I have failed, help will be sent from somewhere else. My faith in the One who will turn the tide is still unshakeable. And whether the tide floods back soon or late, perhaps someone not yet born will read this record of one long gone and through it come to know the Saviour who is the Creator of the universe and the eternal joy of crusty old Doctor Matthew Batchelor.

Even so, come, dear Lord Jesus. Amen.

Historical Note

The theory of evolution pervades our thinking today, whether we realise it or not. Anyone who does not believe it finds it hard to swim against the tide. But the theory is a house of cards and serious flaws were there from the beginning. I have written this story partly to explain how it developed – long before Charles Darwin – and to expose some of those flaws as they might have been seen through contemporary eyes.

In this book the major characters are real people except for Matthew Batchelor himself and Scipio Africanus. I have tried to use their actual words where I can. William Ward, who later became a member of the Serampore Missionary Trio (Carey, Marshman and Ward), was a radical political newspaper editor before his conversion although it is not quite clear whether he was still editing the *Derby Mercury* in 1794. He certainly did write a political address for the Derby Society for Political Information which led to the prosecution of the editors when it was republished in the London paper *The Morning Chronicle*. In fact it is possible that he wrote not one but two addresses delivered in Derby that were later subject to prosecution and acquittal.[1]

Like the other members of the missionary trio, William Ward clearly had an outstanding mind and like them he began life in obscure poverty. Even before his conversion he was a very different sort of character to Erasmus Darwin. They must have known each other, probably quite well, but there is no definite record that remains today of any interaction between them. All the members of the Serampore Missionary Trio were geniuses on the same level as Erasmus Darwin, despite their initial educational handicaps. However, their achievements were not of a type that is now celebrated, except in evangelical circles.

---

[1] Desmond King-Hele speaks of one address. Jonathan Powers distinguishes two and shows a reproduction of both which seem different without precise reference to his sources. The second dates from a meeting held in November 1792. He does not mention Ward. Ward's biographer, Stennett, speaks of two addresses, both defended at law by Erskine. One is the address that was reprinted in *The London Morning Chronicle,* the other the address read in Paris. I have treated them as one in the story to avoid complexity. Perhaps Matthew Batchelor's memory of the events is hazy by 1859!

They spent, or rather sacrificed, their lives boldly promoting the truth in a hostile and dangerous climate. In contrast, Erasmus Darwin spent his in comfort, quietly, almost furtively, promoting a monumental error.

Of the minor figures, Susan, Mrs B, Farmer and Ellen Samuel, Jacob Herrod and his brother as well as a few others are fictional. The banker, Mr Archer, was the real minister of Agard Street Particular Baptist Chapel but his full name in real life was Archer Ward. He was not related to William Ward as far as is known (it was a common Derby surname) so I have dropped "Ward" from his name in the story to avoid confusion. None of his sermons have survived. I have borrowed and adapted passages from sermons by his contemporary, John Ryland, to represent his preaching in the story since these are available and Ryland was from the same denomination. Most of the other minor characters were also real people; the amateur architect Mr Leaper, for instance, was a magistrate related by marriage to Archer Ward.

The story includes many events that actually happened and I have tried to incorporate any details that are known about them. The meeting at the Talbot Inn really took place and the account in the story includes words from William Ward's actual address which was later published. The meeting at Agard Street addressed by the orator John Thelwall is also real and William Ward was responsible for allowing him the use of the chapel without permission. The ensuing riot with chapel windows broken is also a fact. The Grand Trunk Canal is the old name for the canal we now call the Trent and Mersey Canal. Josiah Wedgwood and Erasmus Darwin were prime movers in getting the canal approved by parliament and built.

Parliamentary reform, the abolition of slavery, the early overseas missions, the rise of evolutionary theories, the canal revolution in transport, the ideas of the French Revolution, Deism, Freemasonry – all these things were swirling about and interacting in England in the 1790s in a way that makes it a fascinating period. The influence of evangelical Christianity was the direct cause, indirect cause, unidentified enemy or obvious foe of each of these strands in varying proportions. Each influenced the other in ways that were social, economic and philosophical, producing effects that we can only dimly trace now. Some of the cross currents are surprising: the evangelical poet William Cowper, for instance, was a great admirer of Erasmus Darwin's poetry. Nowadays we would expect our favourite hymn-writers to be more theologically astute – and to have better poetic taste!

Like Matthew Batchelor, I have unshakeable faith that the evolutionary tide will one day turn and I think I begin to see signs of the high water mark – which is why I have written this story. Erasmus Darwin could have had no idea of the sheer complexity of biological substances, a fragile complexity that excludes random beneficial inherited mutations and he would have hoped for the future discovery of millions of transitional fossils that have since not been discovered.

Like Matthew, I am sure that come what may, "truth will out". One day the theory of evolution will be acknowledged for what it is, a convenient Victorian myth for avoiding God, quite unsubstantiated by scientific experiment. I hope this tale has been not only entertaining (and full of historical information if you want to look for it) but helpful to any young (or older) person who loves the Truth or who is groping towards Him.

I include below a list of the major sources I consulted (I also read a lot of Erasmus Darwin's interminable poetry) in preparing this story, in case anyone should want to explore further.

Thanks are due to David Kitching for his expert help with the parts of the story that involve the Trent and Mersey Canal.

BIBLIOGRAPHY

Ivon Asquith, "James Perry and the Morning Chronicle 1790–1821" (PhD thesis, University of London, 1973).

Maxwell Craven, "Great Taste and Much Experience in Building: Richard Leaper: Amateur Architect," *The Georgian Group Journal* 17 (2010): 152–172.

Erasmus Darwin, *Zoonomia* (London: J. Johnson, 1794–1796), 2 vols.

Paula Elizabeth Sophia Dumas, "Defending the Slave Trade and Slavery in Britain in the Era of Abolition, 1783–1833" (PhD thesis, University of Edinburgh, 2012).

Olaudah Equiano, *The Interesting Narrative of the Life of Olaudah Equiano* (London, 1789).

E. Fearn, "The Derbyshire Reform Societies 1791–1793," *Derbyshire Archaeological Journal* 88 (1968): 47–59.

Albert Goodwin, *Friends of Liberty: The English Democratic Movement in the Age of the French Revolution* (London: Hutchinson, 1979).

Thomas Jones Howell, *State Trials and Proceedings for High Treason and Other Crimes and Misdemeanors ... From the Year 1783 to the Present Time* (London,1817), 22:966–1023.

Mark Jones, "The mobilisation of public opinion against the slave trade and slavery: Popular abolitionism in national and regional politics, 1787-1838" (PhD thesis, University of York, 1998).

Desmond King-Hele, *Erasmus Darwin: A Life of Unequalled Achievement* (London: Giles de la Mare Publishers, 1999).

Jean Lindsay, *The Trent and Mersey Canal* (London: David & Charles, 1979).

John Clark Marshman, *Life and Times of Carey, Marshman, and Ward* (London, Longman, Brown, Green, Longmans, & Roberts, 1859).

Thomas Paine, *Rights of Man* (London: Daniel Isaac Eaton, 1795).

Jonathan Powers, *'Evolution' Evolving: Part 1: Dr Erasmus Darwin*, Extended ed. (Derby: Quandary Books, 2020).

Rabaut de Saint-Etienne, *The History of the Revolution of France* (London: J. Debrett, 1792).

The Tribune, A Periodical Publication Consisting Chiefly of the Political Lectures of J. Thelwall (London, 1795), Vol. I.

John Rippon, "An Account of the Particular Baptist Society for Propagating the Gospel Among the Heathen Including a Narrative of its Rise and Plan" in his *The Baptist Annual Register for 1790,1791,1792 and part of 1793* (London, 1793), 371–378.

Nicholas Rogers, "Burning Tom Paine: Loyalism and Counter-Revolution in Britain, 1792–1793," *Histoire sociale / Social History* 32, no 64 (1999): 139–171.

Samuel Stennett, *Memoirs of the Life of the Rev. William Ward* (London: J. Haddon,1825).

R.P. Sturges, "The Membership of the Derby Philosophical Society, 1783–1802," *Midland History* 4, no.3 (1978): 212–229.

GLOSSARY

Aliens Act (1793), an act requiring all foreigners arriving in Britain to be recorded on arrival and to register with a magistrate.

Apothecary, a preparer and supplier of medicines to doctors, surgeons and the general public. Of lower status than physicians but provided medical advice to the general public.

Birmingham Riots (1791), a protest against the spread of French Revolutionary ideas and the efforts of the Deist Joseph Priestly to gain full civil rights for dissenters. Mobs smashed and fired the chapels, businesses and homes of dissenters in Birmingham.

Botany Bay, a destination in Australia for British criminals sentenced to transportation.

Cheque Clerks, canal company officials who worked out the fees chargeable according to the weight and type of cargo on a canal boat.

Cipher, old word for calculate.

Cloths, canvas covers fastened over a canal boat to protect the cargo.

Cut, contemporary slang or dialect word for canal.

Deism, the belief that the nature of God can be deduced by reasoning without relying on any revelation (such as the Bible).

Derby Rib Stocking Machine, a mechanical attachment which enabled a stocking frame to produce stockings in an elastic ribbed stitch.

Etruria, Josiah Wedgwood's Stoke-on-Trent ceramics factory, also his home. Named after the place in Italy where ancient black basalt ware ceramics were found.

Full-bottomed wig, a wig not tied back into a pigtail. A badge of office for doctors, lawyers and parsons.

Georgius Secundus Dei Gratia, "George II by the Grace of God."

Grand Trunk Canal, an early name for the Trent and Mersey Canal.

Habeas Corpus, short for "writ of *Habeas Corpus*", the summons to produce in court someone who has been imprisoned in order to determine whether the imprisonment is lawful.

Indentures, legal agreement to work without pay over a specified period of time in order to learn a trade.

Levelling, (in this context) forcibly reducing society to equality by taking from the rich and giving to the poor.

Lock, a short section on a canal with water-tight gates at both ends into which boats can be drawn in order to travel between sections of a canal at different levels. When the boat is in the lock the gates are closed and the water level is changed to allow the boat to proceed.

Mersey Flat, a double ended barge, often with a sail, used on the River Mersey.

Navigation, (short for "inland navigation") canal.

Ostler, a man who looked after horses at an inn.

Pretender to the Throne, someone claiming to be the rightful ruler of a country ruled by someone else. Queen Anne used the term "Pretender"to refer to her half-brother, James, and it continued to be used of the Stuart claimants to the throne from then onwards.

Radical, someone who advocates thorough political change "from the roots". In this period electoral reform was an important radical issue.

Revolution of 1688 (also known as the Glorious Revolution or the Bloodless Revolution), the deposition of James II and the accession of his daughter and her husband William Prince of Orange as constitutional monarchs. The powers of constitutional monarchs are limited by laws such as the Bill of Rights and the Act of Settlement.

Rippon's Selection, *A Selection of Hymns from the Best Authors, Intended to Be an Appendix to Dr. Watts' Psalms and Hymns*, compiled by John Rippon (1751-1836) and published in 1787. A very widely used and influential hymn book at this time.

Sans-Culottes (literally "without [knee] breeches" i.e. they wore long trousers), the common, lower class people of eighteenth century France, many of whom became supporters of the French Revolution.

Somerset Case (1772), ruled that that it was unlawful to forcibly transport James Somerset, an enslaved African, out of England. The judges ruled: "The state of slavery is ... so odious, that nothing can be suffered to support it but positive law ... I cannot say this case is allowed or approved by the law of England ..." This was considered by many to have declared slavery illegal in England.

Stage, London to Liverpool, regular route by coach from London to Liverpool, stopping to change horses at designated inns en route.

Surgeon, a practitioner who carried out all hands-on treatments such as setting bones and bandaging wounds. Surgeons learned their craft through apprenticeship and were of lower status than physicians.

Towpath, a path alongside a canal or river used by horses drawing boats.

Trinity, one God existing in three Persons.

Turnpike, a road maintained by a trust where tolls for the upkeep of the road were collected at gated points along the route.

Warrant, a legal document signed by a judge or magistrate giving permission to arrest a specific person for a specific reason.

Waybill, a document issued by a carrier precisely describing a vessel's cargo.

DON'T MISS CHRISTINA EASTWOOD'S PREVIOUS BOOKS

HEART OF REBELLION

Tom Alford is being threatened for breaking a rule he did not even know existed. Now he is in the power of an informer who wants him to betray his friend, Nick, who meets with a group of townspeople to read the Bible and pray together. But this is 1685: such meetings are illegal!

WULFGAR THE SAXON

Were the old Saxon gods real? If not, where did everything come from? Wulfgar is perplexed, and sudden death for him and his village seems only too likely, as fierce Viking raiders are over-running his native Wessex. When he least expects it, Wulfgar meets a stranger who gives him surprising answers, but how will he and his friends escape when their turn comes?

Find out more online: **www.ritchiechristianmedia.co.uk**